The Chronicles Of Quinn

Adventures on the High Seas

Barbara Haxby

ISBN: 978-0-9964674-0-7

Edited by Gail Koffman

Photo of turtle and whale tail by E.A.Campbell

Book Design by Dave de la Vega, Elefunt Media

Prologue

Hazel meets Quinn

The night light gently illuminated the small studio apartment. A woman, nearly a centurion, tossed in her covers through various dream states to consciousness. With a deep breath, she opened her eyes and realized she had awoken just past midnight.

Swinging her legs over the side of the bed, she reached for the spectacles on the night stand and carefully stood up. Ignoring the nearby walker, she ambled into the kitchen for a glass of water. Surely after ninety seven years of traveling the globe, living in three different countries, and maintaining her independence after the death of her husband she could make it across the room on her own two feet.

After quenching her thirst, she turned to retrace her steps, when out of the corner of her eye she saw the visage of a man standing next to the couch. Hazel inhaled sharply as fear and surprise jolted her wide awake. An exclamation escaped her lips as she was momentarily frozen. Although he appeared to be of modest age, his face revealed years of exposure to the elements. Green eyes blazed with intensity. Thick tousled red hair contrasted with a sparse beard. Was the man actually shimmering?

Her plastic water cup skittered across the counter as she fumbled for the wall switch and flooded the room with welcome light. Her heart raced in her chest and her skin shivered over her neck and back, but the apparition was gone.

Making her way back to the bed, Hazel sat nervously on the edge. Had she seen a ghost? She struggled to recall details in her mind. The man wore a cream-colored shirt made of extremely durable material. The sleeves were rolled up onto the forearm and laces and toggles secured the front. A satchel hung casually off his shoulder and he held a spear in his hand. She eyed the phone and wondered about calling the front desk. No, she thought, they already think I am crazy. Leaving the room well lit and her glasses perched upon her nose, she pulled the covers past her chin. Eventually, sleep overtook her and the next time she awoke, sunlight was streaming between the blinds.

That morning, Hazel sipped on her coffee as she contemplated the previous evening. She sat on the couch and studied the scrimshaw on the table in front of her. She fondly remembered the trip to Mystic, Connecticut and shopping along the wharf. One of the few historic whaling vessels still afloat, the Charles Morgan, sat moored to the dock as a museum. She and her husband George sauntered around town the entire day and wanted something to commemorate their trip. After examining several items of carved whalebone, they settled on an 8x10 inch piece of scrimshaw which prominently displayed a whaling vessel in full sail. Her mind kept going back to the ethereal visitor and she intuitively felt he was somehow associated with the artwork. Yes, he could have walked right off the deck and into her living room.

With evening approaching, Hazel found herself constantly looking over towards the small table, expecting to see her sailor at every turn. She could think of only two people she could discuss her experience with. Her family would be visiting that weekend. Her grandniece Barbara and her husband Tim would be thrilled with her ghost story. They were into that sort of gibberish. Hazel always smiled politely while grimacing on the inside when they spoke of energy and psychic fairs. Making a decision, she gently wrapped the carving in papers and placed it in a bag under the bathroom sink. Next time they came to visit, she would ask for them to take it to their house.

Barbara and Tim Meet Quinn

I held the scrimshaw in my hands, feeling the coolness of the bone. This came from the head of a whale I thought and tried to envision the animal. The design of the boat was surprisingly intricate and must have been painstakingly carved. Chase crafts were on the hunt in the water and a pod of whales were swimming away in the distance. As I gently traced the riggings under my finger, I closed my eyes and could actually feel the design of the ships. After a moment, I handed it to Tim.

"So what exactly did Hazel say?" Tim held a jewelers glass to his eye as he studied the piece.

"She thinks she saw a ghost." I sat back in the chair and mused. Our luncheon the other day with my aunt had been quite interesting when she somewhat sheepishly recanted her story.

"Do you feel anything?" We had been practicing psychometry, the art of reading the energy surrounding an object to discover facts about an event or person.

"I think we need a couple of drinks to loosen the screws a bit. Make us some margaritas and we will investigate further. Be generous with the tequila and use the good stuff." Tim placed the artifact in his lap and we proceeded to enjoy our refreshments and were soon giggling and relaxed.

"Hold this and tell me what you see or feel." Tim handed over the scrimshaw and turned the lights down low.

I closed my eyes and tried to clear the endless clutter that floats around in my mind. After reflecting for some time, I finally said, "I see a face with a beard and a mark upon the cheek."

"Good, I believe I am getting into the zone now." Tim started to breathe slower and I placed the item back into his hands. After a few moments, he began to channel. "I feel a chilly breeze and the sting of salt. No, I taste the salt of the ocean." Tim slowly licked his lips as he concentrated. "Wow, it is very powerful. I am cold and I can see my breath in front of me before the wind whisks it away. I am a man, maybe in my late twenties but so incredibly old in my soul. There is pain and remorse in my heart. I am part of the crew on a ship. The sails are full of wind and I feel the movement of the boat through the waves."

I was going to ask another question when a sharp pain jabbed on the inside of my left wrist. "Ouch! Oh damn, I'm sorry. I did not mean to pull you out of your trance."

"That's alright. It was starting to slip away. Come to think of it, my wrist is hurting too." Tim rubbed his arm and reached for his glass. "This is interesting but I believe I am tasting rum over the tequila. That must be his drink of choice. We will remember that for next time."

The next week, we chose a quiet evening and cracked open a bottle of Kraken rum, purchased for the picture of the squid on the label. Soon Tim was deep in trance and had the sailor in his mind's eye.

"Are you with us?" I queried as Tim's breathing became accentuated with heavy sighs and he began the process of channeling - communicating with a consciousness existing on a different energy level than our own.

"Yes, I am here." Tim's whisper was hoarse with a different voice quality and his hands reached up to stroke his face. His eyebrows arched in surprise. "What happened to my beard? Where am I? I do not feel the rocking of the sea?"

I calmly introduced myself and attempted to explain as the man channeled through. Sometimes initial meetings could be laced with confusion, fear, and even anger. "You are speaking through somebody else. Do you believe you are alive?" I had to ask the question as sometimes a ghost energy does not realize they had died. When the realization finally hit, the emotions that surrounded the death could be very strong and require time for processing.

Tears welled from Tim's eyes and his voice choked with emotion. "No, I died at sea. Oh my God! Somebody has finally been able to listen. It has been years and years." Deep sobs rocked Tim's shoulders' as he breathed deeply and gained his composure. "I am Quinn Cache and I created the drawing on the scrimshaw."

"Thank you for coming, Quinn. You are safe here. Would you like to speak?" I tried to put our new guest at ease and let him gain his footing. Through trial and error, I had learned not to ask questions too fast.

"I am a member of a whaling crew. Not a profession I would have chosen but that is the truth." Tim's eyes' blinked several times as they attempted to focus.

"Why are you here Quinn?" I asked. "What is it we can do for you?"

"You can tell my story for I have something to share. For only then will I be ready to fully depart."

"Okay. Where do we begin?" I clicked on the voice recorder and began taking notes.

With a smile Tim sat deep in his chair. "Hang on because we are starting our voyage and the seas have a tendency to be rough."

With the lights turned down and a candle flickering, Quinn began to tell his story.

CHAPTER 1

The Capture

Quinn peered intently into the storefront window. The freshly fallen snow illuminated the dark New England night. His feet shuffled slightly as he cramped his toes to keep them warm. Wryly he looked at his shoes. As the son of a cobbler, his own footwear had much to be desired. He had just finished up work for the evening and was en route to meet his brother. The salty scent of the ocean was strong this close to the wharf but Quinn still wrinkled his nose in distain. The smell of death lingered in the breeze from the processing of whales that occurred in the bay. Pulling his thin coat around his neck, he craned his head up and down the street. Where was his brother? They had just spoken earlier that afternoon at the shop and he mentally replayed the conversation.

His sibling had sauntered in and leaned against the work table. "Hey Quinn, I have a job for us tonight," he said.

Quinn was busy pounding a tack into the sole of a shoe. Although far from wealthy, their family owned a respectable cobbler or cordwainer business. When the two oldest boys reached their mid teens they moved out of the family house and worked in town. Quinn chose to stay under the tutelage of his father. Not only was he learning the art of making shoes, but he was also mastering the pen and paper. His brother on the other hand was much more of a free spirit. He took the money where he could get it.

"What kind of work? The last job you rustled up for us was a disaster." Quinn smiled and shook his head at the same time. They had arrived at the site to find a huge mound of debris that was supposed to be gone by morning. Having no horses or wagon, it was impossible and they left empty-handed.

His brother answered in mock distress. "You will never let me forget that one. Okay, I admit that last one was a bad decision. This is just loading supplies for the ships at the dock. Meet me at the bookstore and we'll get a bite to eat before starting."

"Alright, get out of here and let me do my work." Quinn feigned exasperation but watched fondly as his brother left. "I'll be at the bookstore right after sundown," he yelled, as the younger boy exited the building.

A snowflake landed in Quinn's eye, startling him from his thoughts. Finding the street empty he cursed to himself late again. He turned to look at the book before him. His breath made a temporary fog onto the window pane as he studied the leather-bound Bible. The swirls stamped into the cover were quite intricate. "I wonder if I could make that pattern on my shoes?" Hearing the crunch of footsteps in the snow, Quinn breathed a sigh of both irritation and relief. "Where have you been, I am starting to freeze out here?" he asked, still studying the tome before him.

The silhouette of a street lantern reflected in the glass and Quinn switched his focus and gazed at his own mirror image. Red hair and the start of mustache mimicking the transformation to manhood stared back at him. With surprise, he realized the approaching footsteps did not belong to his brother, but rather to a stocky man with grey hair and a clean-shaven face. Facing the window but watching the figure loom behind him, Quinn surged with adrenaline as the man uncovered a large stick from beneath his coat. Quickly spinning on his heel, the boy almost faced his assailant before the wood struck his temple. Pain ricocheted through his head and his vision blurred as he fell hard to the street.

The heavy-set man furtively glanced around to make sure he was not observed. Grabbing the jacket around the boy's neck, he quickly hoisted him over his shoulder and strode across the street and into the side entrance of a tavern. Dropping him onto the floor in a back room, he expertly bound his hands and feet with hemp.

A second man wearing fancy clothes and a square hat entered the storeroom. "Did you get a healthy one that is young? The boat is getting ready to set out and needs more hands. They rejected that other guy, said he was too old."

"Aye, this one should be prime. But the daft boy turned right as I hit him." Using his foot, he nudged the prone form over and shook his head as he noted the blood coming from the wound beside the bushy red eyebrow. "He's still breathing so he must be alive. This one was right across the street looking in the bookstore. I did not even have to go into the alleys." The man was quite pleased with himself.

The owner of the bar kneeled down and studied the new arrival. "Sorry my boy, but I've got a business to run and you have become a profitable commodity," he whispered into his unconscious ear.

"Yea, thanks to the Boston whaling industry. Too many boats, poor pay, not enough crew, and lots of demand." The burly man nonchalantly shrugged his shoulders. "I better get this one to the docks before he wakes up."

The man wrapped Quinn in a blanket, and while stowing him amongst the barrels in the back of a wagon, noticed another older boy trotting down the street. He eyed him hungrily and wondered if he would have time to get another. Pretending to fix the collar of his coat, he waited momentarily as the newcomer stopped right in front of the bookstore, as a large group of sailors arrived from the docks. Some of the men entered the drinking establishment while a few chatted at the entrance. Setting his club onto the floorboard, he was quite vexed as he hoisted himself into the seat. He did not have time to wait for a clear opportunity and snapped the lines over the back of the horse.

Quinn's brother arrived at the store window. "Wow," he thought, "maybe I am not late after all." The boy was perplexed when Quinn did not show. He called to the men across the street. "Hey, did you guys see a tall red-haired kid over here?" They replied in the negative. Did he choose not to come? he wondered. No, he always did what he said. Looking to the new cover of snow, he could see some spots that looked like blood. Kneeling down, he could see two sets of prints and a flattened area. As time passed, he grew more and more uneasy. The smell of cooking whale oil filled him with foreboding. Finally with a small seed of fear starting to bloom in the pit of his abdomen, he set out in search of his brother.

The horse and wagon traveled to a designated pier. Pulling up to a chase boat tied to the dock, the man disembarked from the seat and walked to the back and unfolded the blanket. Three sailors standing at the edge came over.

"He has blood all over his head." A bearded face scowled with disapproval as he leaned close to assess the new arrival. A heavily calloused hand turned the boy's head towards the light and lifted up the lips to check the teeth.

The tavern employee stepped backwards as the scent of sweat, salt, and whale permeated his nostrils. "How do you think I get them? Men are not exactly standing in line to serve on your ships and those that are able have run off to California. This one was looking at the books so he may be smart." He looked to the sailors before him and shrugged when they did not appear impressed, but he knew he had the upper hand. The crimps controlled the flow of workers. "He's thin but looks healthy enough. Has all his fingers and toes and Boss said he should be worth top dollar."

A small moan escaped Quinn's lips as the lead sailor lifted the blanket to get a better look. "Okay, we'll take him."

Relieved, the wagon driver pocketed the money. "How long you gone this time?" The whaling boats could be gone weeks to years depending on how far they ranged. This particular crew manned a bark that could process at sea.

"I don't know. The whales are getting harder to find. They are not close to shore anymore and we might go weeks without even sighting one. By the look of the supplies the company has delivered we may be gone awhile."

"Well then, until next time." The bar employee quickly returned back onto the wagon seat and the group split company. The whalers looked around cautiously and boarded their boat, placing Quinn at their feet among the supplies. Taking an oar, they returned to the mother ship.

CHAPTER 2

Awakening in the Hold

Terrible pain in his head finally roused Quinn from his stupor. Bile rose in his throat as he realized he was gently rolling back and forth. Was he in a boat? Dried blood matted his hair and he struggled to clear the fog from his thoughts. He tried to wipe his eyes, only to discover his hands and feet were bound. Panicking, he began to thrash against the ties which bit deeply past the top layer of his skin. Exhausted, he heaved as he tried to connect fragments of his last memories. The bookstore, his brother, the man's visage in the window danced in his mind. He wondered if he had died and was in hell. Yet he breathed, and he hurt very badly.

Quieting, eventually he was able to make out shapes beside him in the darkness. Other forms were lying prone on the floor. The hemp rope binding his wrists had become saturated with his own blood. He could hear the sounds of water lapping up against the creaking timber. The planks beneath his cheek permeated with the smell of tar.

Fear consumed him and he started to shiver uncontrollably. Soft whimpering could be heard in the background and the scent of human defecation finally registered in his nostrils. No longer able to contain the nausea, Quinn retched over and over. His mouth was sticky and dry and he wondered how long it had been since he had eaten or drank. Terrified, he closed his eyes tightly, praying this was a dream.

"Are you okay?" A trembling young whisper directly next to Quinn spoke up. "God this feeling is horrible. I cannot stop throwing up myself. I'm George." His voice was ragged with dehydration and emotion. "My father told me not to hang out near the docks. I was just trying to find him." Gentle sobs choked his words.

Quinn's reply was cut short when heavy hinges squealed as the hatch to the hold swung open. Quinn gasped as wraith-like shadows were cast eerily onto the wall. Fearing the worst, he was surprised as two men came down the ladder carrying buckets. Their lantern emitted a distinctive smell and in the flickering light Quinn could finally recognize they were in the deepest level of the boat. The boys were lying shoulder to shoulder, most already shackled by leg and arm irons. The men were busy examining each of the newest arrivals.

"Damn that bar man, this one is already gone. The Captain will not be pleased." A boot pushed the lifeless form and the body was stabbed with a sharp stick for verification before moving onto the next. "Are you still with us?" The man knelt down and shook one of the new abductees on the shoulder. When awake, they poured water from the bucket down his throat. Swiftly drawing a knife, they cut the hemp tie and secured one wrist and one ankle with a set of irons attached to a wooden beam.

One by one, they worked their way towards Quinn who was relieved to recognize they were actual men and not demons as he feared. The red-haired boy looked into the eyes of the two men. A cloth soaked with seawater was tied around their faces. "Where am I? Why have I been taken?"

The captors looked at each other and laughed. "Don't you know? You are going to be a whaler."

"But I don't want to be a whaler." Quinn tugged at his ropes as they cut his bonds but they easily pinned him to the wooden floor.

"Lay still or I'll slit you," the man sneered in his ear. "I hope you change your mind. We are miles from shore and the water's very cold and real deep. A straight shot to the abyss of Davy Jones' Locker."

Quinn's wrist and ankle were quickly secured and he was left inhaling the oddly sweet smell of iron. The small amount of water quenched his thirst, but the sickening roll of the boat threatened to evict his precious hydration. The men finished their rounds and returned above, leaving the boys once again in the dark. Quinn shivered on the cool floor while he willed his numb arms to move. "Well, at least I am getting some feeling again in my fingers," he thought. He rubbed his raw wrist with his free hand and gingerly probed the matted hair on his head. The sharp pain evoked the intense vision of the sturdy man bringing his wooden club to bear. The young boy next to him was coughing, and Quinn had noted some dried blood on his lips when the lantern was nearby.

"Hey George, are you okay? You don't sound good." Quinn whispered very quietly, still not sure if talking was allowed. "I'm Quinn, by the way."

"Oh Quinn, I am so scared. I am not okay," George answered. "The doctor said I have a breathing problem around dust and dirt, and my ribs hurt terribly. The man dropped me coming down the stairs. I feel like a weight is on my chest."

Quinn cocked his head towards his neighbor and listened as each breath was accompanied with a wheeze. A tinge of regret rushed through him as he thought of his younger brother and he felt an immediate rapport with lad next to him. Although he was terrified himself, he found himself feeling protective of his new friend.

"Do you think they are going to sell us as slaves?" The younger boy's voice quivered with concern and fear.

Quinn pondered the question. He was now fully convinced that he and his new brethren had been shanghaied. He had heard stories of men disappearing. Hundreds of boats now frequented the whaling ports and the gold rush had drawn many able men westward. Not for a moment did he consider that he himself would have been a target. He shook his head at his naïveté and a pit of fear blossomed for his own brother. Had they gone after him as well?

"I think they took us to work on the boat. My grandpa said there is a shortage of sailors. I thought they were using prisoners to fill their quotas." A voice from Quinn's opposite side added in the conversation. "I'm Jonas. I think I have been here a few days. I have lost track."

"How long do we have to stay here?" George asked.

"I don't know, hopefully not long." Quinn gave a whisper of encouragement even though his own heart churned with dismay and dread.

Minutes turned to hours which followed into days. Buckets of water and a food-like substance were brought around at unknown intervals. No facility existed to relieve oneself. At first, bodily functions were minimal due to lack of nourishment. But as time passed, the smell of excrement became overpowering. Their captors openly cursed at their duty and hurried through their routine. If a boy was not conscious enough to take nourishment, they were passed over.

While weakness dulled his thoughts, Quinn slipped in and out of consciousness and prayed for death. Talking amongst the group had lessened dramatically and then ceased all together. George, the ailing boy next to him had not responded to his query for some time. During the last visit by the captors, he had tried to encourage the younger boy to take water but he had refused. He did not speak, but his innocent eyes locked with Quinn's and he shook his head no.

In the squalid darkness, Quinn was aroused to awareness when he no longer heard the raspy breath of his neighbor and weakly called George's name. Not hearing a response, he turned onto his side and gazed in amazement as a glowing form began to manifest before him. He rubbed the dried matter from his eyes as he struggled to focus and comprehend what he was seeing. An angel was touching the dying boy on the shoulder. She was beautiful. The lines of her body and the feathers of her wings were backlit by the sun even though no such light shone down here. Quinn reached over to her with his shackled hand. "Please, take me too, I beg you."

She turned to look at him and a melodic voice responded. "I am sorry, but it is not your time yet."

With a sorrowful smile, the apparition disappeared and Quinn realized that not only was he shivering but that every hair on his body was erect. George had stopped moving altogether and Quinn knew the boy was dead. He trembled with anger. First he burned at the younger boy's abduction as well as his own. What right did they have to take such a youngster? They had undoubtedly injured him gravely which contributed to his death. His thoughts turned to despair when he thought of the angel. Why didn't she take him as well? He could barely go on. In his frustration, he started to cry but the tears did little more than moisten the dirt on his lashes and make his eyes stick together. Desperate, he held his breath until almost blacking out, but found it impossible to facilitate his own passing.

After several minutes, his breathing started to settle and he thought back to the angel. Who was that beautiful creature? Growing up, he had dutifully gone to church every Sunday but did not consider himself a religious person. For the first time however, he knew there was something beyond the life that he knew. He felt a small amount of peace for George, as the boy had been in so much pain. He realized he felt a sliver of hope for himself as well. There was a path that even their captors could not control. He tried to fall back asleep as he sensed the angel would not be returning soon.

Although the boys were no longer aware of time, almost two weeks had passed when a new man came into the hold. Only eight of the boys remained. The process was a matter of attrition, where only the strongest survived. The man had an official air about him, and the now familiar captors flanked him on either side. Kneeling down at the first captive, he asked, "Would you like to be released and join the service of the crew?"

The first boy begged to be released and go home. Stepping over him, the mate approached the next frail form and asked the same question. This boy wisely answered "Yes." Anything seemed a reasonable alternative to the current condition. A deprogramming procedure deployed by many military institutions seemed to be followed on the ship —a process of stripping one down to the bare minimum and then building them back up into a team player. The first volunteer was released from his shackles and assisted from the bottom of the ship and disappeared up the steps.

Soon the man came to Quinn and asked for his response. "Oh yes, please, I want to join the crew." He tried to forcefully accept but only a whisper came out.

With his shackles released, Quinn was grasped under his arms and helped to his feet. He attempted to stand and immediately fell to his knees. His ribs showed painfully under his tattered and dirty shirt and his pants fell past his hips. He raggedly inhaled as the exertions caused him to become short of breath. On his hands and knees, he crawled up the decks to his new life on the high seas.

CHAPTER 3

Becoming a Whaler 

he spray of saltwater peppered him hard in the face and was never so welcome. His heart pounded in his chest as he grappled to the gangway to join the rest of the boys. Collapsing onto his back, Quinn glanced around for his companions. "Jonas, you made it," he said weakly to his friend. Relieved, he watched the rest of the boys emerge from the hold and soon they were huddled together for warmth.

Rubbing his body with his free hands, Quinn lay upon the deck. It was dark but the moon was visible beyond the sail. Perhaps that was a good thing, for surely the light of full day would have blinded him. Thirsty and his muscles cramping, he felt terrible. His face was caked and dirty and his hair matted as he ran his hands over his head.

"I am so sorry father, I have failed you. I am so sorry I let them take me, but I am alive." He muttered to himself through quiet tears.

Wind rippled through drawn sails and although the stench of matter still reeked in his clothing, the fresh air was incredibly welcome. A now familiar scent wafted on the air.

"What is that scent?" He smelled oil in the air, similar to coal but different. His nose wrinkled at the strong odor.

"That's whale oil boy, lampers." One of the sailors had approached the group with a cart and handed out bowls of hot soup and some bread.

Another man came over with an armful of used garments. "Here are some new clothes. Throw yours over the side." Then he placed a bundle of torn and tattered pieces of sail on the ground.

"You'll sleep on deck for the time being. Use these sails for a blanket and stay over there out of the wind. Don't lose your cover."

Quinn lifted the bowl to his chapped lips and felt the hot liquid stream into his stomach. He was oddly surprised when the small amount of bread quelled his hunger pains. The boys stripped bare in the chilly breeze to clean themselves and rummage through the pile of clothes to find something that might fit. Rope belts were pulled tight to keep their pants from falling to their knees.

As they passed by small burning drums of oil, many of the crew members studied the new arrivals. Some nodded their heads with a subtle greeting. The air was crisp but immensely preferable to the hold underneath. The boys wrapped themselves in the stiff piece of sail given to them. Shoulder to shoulder and in the protection of some crates, they shared body warmth as it became painfully apparent that a hierarchy existed to be closest to the fires. One by one, uneasy dreams overtook them as they prepared for their first days as whalers.

Quinn awoke early, having spent a restless night trying to stay warm in the frigid temperatures. He wondered if he had been cursed. How do these men believe that this is a way of life? Trying to think of anything to forget the bone-chilling cold, he concentrated on the clicks of the huge steering wheel as the man of the watch kept the rudder amidships. Pink and orange rays appeared far in the horizon which slowly turned into blue sky.

The ship herself seemed to yawn as the crew started to get up for the morning. Looking around, he was surprised how many whalers slept on the deck out in the elements. The new recruits were shown where to stow their few belongings and ordered to get at the end of the line which had formed in front of the galley door for the morning meal. Hierarchy seemed to be the underlying current of order on the ship. Men started moving around, unfurling sail, and organizing rope as the ship started to move in the sea. Looking for any recognizable land mass, Quinn swallowed hard as he noted ocean on all sides.

"Your name?" a man asked, holding an official ships register. The mate had thin blond hair tied back and a patchy beard. "What are you called by?"

Startled out of his observations, Quinn panicked for a moment. Benjamin Quincy Cache was his full name, but would sharing that information put his family at risk? "I go by Quinn," he told the man who jotted down the information and moved on to the next boy.

Suddenly the quiet bantering stopped and sailors moved aside. Expecting the Captain of the boat, the boys were surprised when four men sauntered confidently onto the deck. The crew nodded with respect and adoration as they passed by.

"Who are they?" the boys asked in unison.

"Those are the harpooners." A heavy-set whaler came over to the group. He smiled as he studied the proud men moving across the deck. "It's rumored they sleep with their spears draped across their chests. They are like royalty, other than the Captain and his officers. I'm Rollo." He introduced himself with a toothless smile and pointed to a large furnace in the middle of the ship. Twin iron kettles were surrounded by bricks. A water bath was suspended underneath the apparatus. "After you eat your meal, meet me over by the boiler."

The boys were the last to be served the fish soup and bread. Eating rapidly, Quinn was surprised at how hungry he was. Standing out of the way, they watched the organized chaos as the men unfurled the sails and the ship began to move in the sea.

Rollo waved to them to come over. "Okay, this is your first job. It's very important, because if not done correctly we could sink and as you can see, we are far from land." He smiled as the group before him visibly blanched. Huge permanently blackened hands motioned for the boys to each take a bucket and paddle that he had placed on the deck. After placing a clump of tar from a burlap sack into each container, Rollo used a metal cup attached to a long bar to scoop some whale oil from the large kettle and instructed them to mix the contents together.

"Jeremy will take you below and explain the procedure." He looked at the bedraggled group. Most of them could barely stand up and their new clothing dangled from bony shoulders. "Don't worry," he said gently, "today will be a short day."

"This way," yelled the new man as he motioned them back down into the bowels of the ship. Soon they were back in darkness as the oil lamps cast eerie shadows on the wooden walls. Leading them to the side of the boat he stopped to explain. "Once we are under way, small leaks will become visible. The seal between the planks need constant upkeep."

Carefully studying the sidewall, a drip of seawater trickled down as if on cue. Identifying the source, he took the paddle and carefully pressed the tar mixture into the crevice. "Make sure the hole is filled before you move on to the next board."

"You have got to be kidding," Jonas grimaced to his shipmates. The thought of spending hours on end in the flickering shadows looking for leaks did not appeal to him.

"Well, I would suggest getting started," the crew member chastised. "Any one refusing work gets escorted off the ship."

"Would they let us go home?" Jonas' mind was already churning with possibility.

The sailor seemed to consider the question and smiled without humor or warmth. "No, they run you through with a sword and toss you overboard. Watch your lanterns carefully and I'll be back later to get you."

Feeling the blood run from their faces, the boys quickly got to work, eager to prove their worth. Jonas and Quinn paired off together. They took turns with one holding the light and the other patching.

"I cannot believe we are back down here again." Jonas was somewhat older than Quinn and the quickest of the group to voice his opinion. "My arms are so weak I am actually shaking. Tell me about yourself, Quinn. What's your fancy?"

"I grew up in the country, but my brother and I moved into town after my mother passed and my father remarried." Quinn loved the solitude of the shop at night. Once his father left for the evening to return to the outskirts of town, he would sit by the lamp and read books. "I once thought I would become a writer."

"Ohh – a learned man are we? Well, I won't hold it against you." Jonas gently chided him. "What were you doing near the docks?"

"My brother had arranged a job for us to a bit of extra money." Quinn gave over the lantern and started to patch instead. "I only got a glimpse of the man who hit me. He had short hair, was heavy-set and wore a large dark overcoat. The next thing I remember was waking up here."

"Those damn crimpers. That particular one works in the bar. You know the one with the huge wooden doors and the sign that has the crossed balers." Jonas growled with contempt.

"Oh, you mean the long-handled ladles that Rollo was using today? How do you know he works out of there? The bookstore is just up the street. I was foolishly looking through the window and not paying attention." Quinn had replayed this scene in his mind a hundred times.

"Well, I frequented the taverns a bit," Jonas shrugged nonchalantly. "My father got me started early on the taste of the drink. Plus they make a pretty good stew there. I had stopped in for a bite and that particular man asked me what bark I was assigned too. I guess I was pretty cocky when I told him I was a landlubber and proud of it. Come to think of it, he kept filling my glass. Pretty soon I was a bit sauced when he asked if I wanted to pay for part of my meal by moving some heavy bags. And the rest is history."

Quinn chuckled at his companion who reminded him of his brother. Jonas' ability to take this new adventure in stride and still maintain his spirit made him jealous. He found himself thinking of the angel and concentrated on his memory of her. If she came for him, he would welcome the journey. After what seemed an eternity, one of the whalers called them up. Moving up a new set of stairs, they found themselves on an entirely new floor of the boat.

"Wow, is that a canon?" one of the boys asked. They had just passed an apparatus that was aimed out a closed porthole. "Are we going to war?"

"It's more like a punt gun. Not quite as large. We might fire on another ship but usually they are used for signaling. But believe me, there are pirates out there. Some of them are from other whaling companies." The whaler seemed to laugh at his own joke.

Although they had only worked for a few hours, Quinn was both famished and tired to the bone. After eating their soup and bread, the boys wrapped themselves in the torn pieces of sail and loitered around the kettle pots, listening to the seasoned whalers speak amongst themselves. Largely ignored, they were at least not run off. He pulled the stiff material up around his head, covering his exposed ears. The crisp wind freely tousled his closely cropped hair. Perhaps longer locks were in order if he were to survive this ordeal. With his belly full and his new friends next to him, Quinn slept that night, neither waking nor dreaming.

CHAPTER 4

The First Whale

After weeks and perhaps even months of settling into the routine, the new recruits were busy patching the cracks in the bottom of the ship. It seemed to be a never-ending process. Where as one day a section was bone dry, the next moment water would trickle into a small puddle.

"Boys, you are needed up on the gangway, starboard side," a large voice boomed from above.

Excited at the prospect of having their monotonous duty interrupted, they pushed past each other as they clamored up the steps. The boys burst into the light and Quinn closed his eyes as the sun caressed his face. They usually worked below deck from early morning till dawn, even taking their meals below by the light of the lantern.

"Oh my god, the sky looks so good," Quinn mused as he brought up the end of the line.

Directed around the corner, some of the boys gasped in union and Quinn craned his head around Jonas' taller set of shoulders in front of him. "What is it?" He could not see what had intrigued the group.

"It's a whale!" the front boy yelled back.

The sea of bodies parted and Quinn stopped short as he joined the circle. The head of the great beast lay before him. It was already severed from the body and had just been pulled from the water with the huge block and tackle. He had never seen one up close. It was massive and blood continued to pour unceremoniously from its bulk. He was mesmerized as he stared into the surprisingly large eye which appeared milky and opalescent in death. As the head was hoisted upwards, he could see a lance point being removed from the other eye.

"This particular whale is a good catch, a sperm whale. They are preparing to open the case, that's the portion of the head there. That's where the liquid gold of whaling is found, the spermaceti." One of the whalers had come up behind the group.

Quinn felt his breath hitch as bile rose into his throat and he panicked at the thought of losing his breakfast in front of the entire crew. Tearing his gaze away, he concentrated on his crew mates. They seemed unperturbed by the carnage in front of them. He struggled with his internal emotions, remembering how he was always somehow otherwise occupied when it came to the killing and butchering of any of the farm animals during his boyhood. He had purposely planned on a career that would keep him in the shop all day and able to avoid some of the manual labors he detested.

A wrinkled hand touched him on the shoulder. "You going to be okay?" A voice pierced Quinn's thoughts as the fingers increased in pressure and he actually felt dizzy when he looked at the older man. He had seen him at the fires, but had never actually spoken to him. Isaac pursed his brow as he looked into the red-haired boy's eyes, watching him clench his jaw as he struggled to squash a myriad of emotions. The whaler smiled knowingly and his rough palm gently folded the boys' lifeless hand around the handle of a long blade.

A section of the bulwark had been removed and a wooden cutting stage now hung precariously over the side. Tethered to the vessel was the missing body of the whale. Men were suspended by ropes and balanced on wooden beams, using wide blades on long handles to cut the blubber into sections. Taking a large hook attached to a block and tackle, they secured the leading edge. The whale gently spun in the water and soon long thick sheets of whale hide were being peeled from the carcass and fed to the blubber room below where the boys were now directed.

"You need to cut the flesh into blocks so they can be stacked for further mincing and cooking. We have to get the flesh off the whale as fast as possible before the sharks get too aggressive." The whaler took the blade and showed the group the desired size.

Stepping close to the blankets of whale flesh, Quinn pierced into the side and started to cut as ordered. The skin was incredibly tough, and even though the instrument was sharp, he found himself slipping to his knees as the floor became slick with blood and blubber. His hands slipped on the long handle of the blade, and his constant wiping of his palms on his pants made them wet and stick to his thighs. Soon he was sweating profusely and breathing through his mouth from both exertion and to avoid the stench of death.

Isaac lingered around the group providing instruction as the work progressed. "I need somebody to help the smithy furbish the tools. You," he pointed to Quinn. "Gather any irons and used blades and follow me."

With a handful of instruments under his arm, Quinn was grateful for the opportunity to leave the processing deck. Entering the blacksmith section of the boat, he felt some of his equilibrium returning. The scent of whale fat permeated every pore of his skin. He had wiped the sweat from his eyes, only to find them blurred with oil. He thought back to the whale. That great eye seemed to bore into his soul and openly chastise him and he felt shame and regret. He sat down heavily and started to clean the tools and the memories of the great beast receded as he finally was able to concentrate on the job at hand. He had been responsible for caring for all the tools in his father's shop and examined each one with some expertise.

"This point is weak near the tip," he noted, picking up the iron that was dissected from the lung of the animal. He held the harpoon in his hand, tapping and feeling the metal.

The smithy took the piece from Quinn and studied it. Sure

enough, the boy was right. He looked upon him with appreciative eyes. "You know your metals?"

"I was in charge of keeping all of the equipment in working order back home. I even made some of my own tools." For the first time, Quinn felt some semblance of familiarity and even pride.

"Well, we need to work through that entire pile over there." The smithy leaned back and massaged his knuckles, pleased to let the boy continue his work.

Quinn worked side by side with the smithy and was surprised when the sun cast shadows across the deck. He did not realize he had worked through the entire afternoon. "Oh my gosh. I never returned with the other boys down below. Will the Captain be mad at me?"

"Nope. Besides, I think you just got a promotion out of the depths. Go on, you can join your friends now and get some dinner." Smithy had a genuine smile on his face.

Quinn walked out onto the gangway to the larboard side, away from any processing and waited for his crewmates as the ship was readied for the evening. He was not sure if they continued to work on the whale, or had been sent back below.

"You are different from the others," a voice whispered from behind him. Quinn looked around to see Isaac had materialized at his shoulder. "You can feel the beasts' pain. A most unfortunate gift for a whaler."

Quinn lowered his head as the memory of the whale roared back into his thoughts. His mother had always told him he was extra sensitive. At the time he laughed at the comment, but the rush of remorse he felt when slicing the flesh of the great animal had totally blindsided him earlier this morning. He peered into the man's eyes and both embarrassment and resignation clouded his features.

"It will get better with time. By the way, my name is Isaac. Some advice for you and your friends - at any opportunity, take the whale oil and rub your hands and feet to keep them soft. It also helps keep frostbite away. Without hands and feet, you are no good as a whaler or a member of the crew. Oh - and no matter how cold you are, never make a fire without permission. That is a punishment that can earn the death penalty."

"Thank you, Isaac. I will tell the others." Quinn watched as the man nodded curtly and walked away.

Footsteps sounded behind him as the rest of the boys exploded from below deck. "Where were you? Are you okay?" Quinn's friends appeared concerned at his absence.

"I worked all afternoon in the blacksmith shop cleaning and working on the tools." Quinn looked refreshed from earlier in the day.

"Good thing. Gees, you looked like a sick dog while working on the whale. I thought you were going to faint." Jonas came under his arm in a gesture of helping him stand. All the boys laughed and took turns mimicking Quinn as he labored on the whale.

Quinn smiled as the boys cajoled him. "Come on, I'm hungry. Let's get some chow and drink." The boys joined the line, laughing and joking with each other. After the meal, they settled in to sleep on the deck as always. However, they were closer to the fires and actually mingled with the crew.

CHAPTER 5

Chef

The next morning Quinn was called out as they went to gather their buckets of tar mixture. "You," Rollo boomed as he pointed to Quinn, "Report to the galley. The rest of you, down you go."

The other boys in the group glanced at Quinn, giving him the appreciative thumbs up sign as well as breathing a sigh of envy as he followed Rollo to meet the chef. Walking towards the stern of the boat, they stood in front of the half door as a burly man with dark red hair and a stylish mustache was busy shouting orders to men who were filling pots with water and opening bags of salted fish. Stroking his chin, the Chef turned to examine the new young man standing in front of him.

"Smithy tells me you are talented. I need someone to keep my equipment in shape and help me in the kitchen. What are you good at besides tending tools? Have you ever cooked?"

"Well, no." Quinn could see the cook was sizing him up from head to toe and he tried to dredge up some worthy experience in the kitchen but had none to offer. "But I have been a journeyman in my father's shoe shop for a few years now. I was also learning to read and write."

"Really?" Chef was surprised. They had an educated boy and did not even know it. Other than the officers, very few whalers had the skill. "Read me that list," the cook commanded as he handed him a clipboard.

Quinn read down the page and Chef smiled. Glancing at his friendly face and twinkling eye, Quinn felt for the first time that he might be able to fit into the crew. Seeing the sun and clouds during the day certainly also buoyed the spirits. He felt bad about the other boys being down below but was grateful for this new job, especially if it kept him off the processing crew.

The Chef waved Rollo off and took Quinn by the shoulder. "So over here is the cutlery and the pots are stored underneath. Everything needs to be secured in case of rogue waves and bad weather." He moved over to several scabbards attached to the wall. "Most important are the knives. There's nothing like flying blades to make one move their bowels," he laughed heartily. "Those that do not go on the wall get placed in these boxes, with the pin through the latch. These blades need sharpening and some of the handles are loose. I also want you to check inventory against the roster."

He led him to a small room off the galley. "Here are your tools, and you can sleep here if you like as well. Keep a close eye on the special rum for the officers. It has a tendency to disappear." He thumped the young man on the back and was pleased with his new assistant. "You can get started. I'll need help serving the meals later today. Oh, and by the way, call me Pixie." An incredibly mischievous smile crossed his lips and a bellow escaped him as he turned to finish his preparations.

Quinn surveyed his surroundings and his mind was spinning trying to remember the orders the Chef had just ranted off. Pixie? What kind of name was that? He could actually have a cot to sleep in? He would have his own space? The boys would be green with envy. The large-framed man looked friendly enough but muscular arms looked like he could break a man's' neck with his bare hands. Diving into his new job with enthusiasm not felt for months, he started to take inventory of his supplies until Pixie called to him for assistance.

"Put this on and wash your hands." Chef tossed a clean jacket for Quinn to put on over his shirt. "The officers eat in the room just off the galley. We need to set the table and get ready for the meal. They are served before the other men." Taking a pitcher from the wall, he handed it to Quinn and pointed to the containers along the floor. "Make sure you use the rum in the barrel to the left. Shhhhh- the rum on the right is watered down for the rest of the crew. That way we conserve water and rum, and the men get a bit of drink to keep the scurvy away."

In the dining room, Quinn admired the fine china as he placed the settings. He had not seen actual silverware since his arrival on the boat. He used his fingers to eat in the beginning, and eventually whittled some pieces of spare wood into makeshift forks and spoons. Then he made pieces for all of the other boys and soon some of the seasoned sailors asked him for items. Even Isaac, the most proficient carver on the ship had commented on a few of his pieces.

Carefully filling the glasses with the reserve rum, Quinn quivered with excitement as the officers began to stroll in. He had barely seen the upper echelon of the whaling crew as most of his time thus far was spent below deck. After the mates had taken their seats, the Captain entered the room. All the men briefly stood as he sat at the head of the table. He was older, with a full beard and head of hair. Although his face was weathered by sea and sun, his eyes remained crisp. Quinn mused at the power of the man. On a whaling boat, the captain was both judge and jury, with full autonomy to decide the fate of any man under his command.

A tall man sat at the opposite end of the table that Quinn recognized as the doctor. All the boys had undergone a cursory examination in the first days after their release from the hold. A clean-shaven face, prominent brow, and long grey hair tied smartly behind his head conveyed a stately and precise appearance. His dress was sophisticated and clearly civilian. He warmly greeted the Captain and clearly they were friends but he refrained from the boisterous conversation that soon engrossed the staff in general.

Quinn nervously looked at the bench of condiments in front of him, going over the instructions Pixie had repeated several times.

Expecting the Chef to take the lead in serving, he had to stifle a gasp when the cook sat at the last spot on the table next to the doctor. After the initial greetings, the men discussed the ship's progress, barrels of whale oil secured, and business in general. Quinn hovered in the corner, quickly coming to the table when called upon.

"Who is your new assistant, Pixie?" the doctor queried the Chef.

"Ahh, this boy is from the batch of our newest recruits. He impressed the Smithy yesterday with his skill with the tools. He was a journeyman at his father's cobbler shop." Pixie leaned over and said more quietly under his breath. "He can read and write as well."

"What's your name, son?" the doctor directly addressed Quinn.

Quinn quickly introduced himself and was stunned that he had been addressed at all.

"Perhaps you can come to my office later. I have some tools that need some fine repair." The doctor appeared genuine in his offer.

"Yes sir, I would like that very much." Quinn glanced furtively at Chef who grinned back at him. Although ignored during the rest of the meal, he felt giddy with recognition. Afterwards, he removed all the dishware to the kitchen for cleaning. He looked at the Chef with a newfound respect when he was back in the galley. "Wow, I was not aware you sat with the Captain. Is that usual?"

"Goodness, no. But Captain Eligh is different than the rest. He is the best Master I have sailed with. He knows how to make a man feel appreciated. He honored me by inviting me to his table and I make sure he is taken care of every day. I'll finish up here and you go see what the good doctor has in mind for you." Pixie took a flask and tossed it to Quinn as he exited. "Make sure he gets this, for medicinal purposes."

Quinn finished stowing the last of the cutlery and set off towards the infirmary which was almost directly below them on the next level. He had been advised by the other whalers that having a doctor on board was unusual. The Captain normally acted as the caretaker for the ill and injured, even if not skilled to do so. All ships were required to have a working medicine chest and a copy of the Sailor's Physician for guidance. He felt lucky to have actual trained medical personnel on board. Walking past the ordinates' room, the powder monkeys enviously eyed the flask he carried. These men were responsible for keeping their explosive kegs in order. Outside the infirmary door, Quinn gently knocked.

"Come in," called the voice from inside.

"Hello doctor, you sent for me?" Quinn glanced around, taking in the surroundings. A candle globe sat on the table. The lamp was shorter than normal and contained a reflector which amplified the light.

The man was sitting at his desk writing in his log. Peering above reading glasses perched on the bridge of his nose, he stopped to study the red-haired boy in front of him. "I have some instruments that need sharpening and some hinges that need adjustment. The tools are delicate. Let me show you and make sure you are up to the task."

Leading him to a cabinet, the doctor opened the rough wooden door. Rows of tools hung vertically between pegs driven into the back wall. Quinn's eyes opened in amazement as he studied hooks that terminated in flat plates, various clamps and many different lengths of forceps. A light breeze rustled his hair and he realized that the doctors' room had a porthole window that opened to the outside. Quinn noted several containers under the window on a shelf filled with what looked like leaves and small vials. He peered at the doctor who offered no explanation.

Embarrassed, he quickly dropped eye contact. "My fathers' tools were very delicate. I am sure I can handle what you need. Which ones shall I start with?"

The doctor gathered a few pieces. "Take your time and bring them back when you're done" he instructed. "Is that for me?" He gestured to the flask held tight in Quinn's hand.

"Oh, yes, I meant to give this to you right away." Quinn quickly handed over the rum. "Chef said to make sure you knew it was the good stuff."

Gathering the tools, he headed back to the galley. Seeing his friends on the gangway, he stopped to chat with them. He told them of his day, and shared that he was to sleep in the galley now. Although excited, he did not want to seem boastful.

"You lucky dog. You get to sleep in a room?" Jonas seemed a bit despondent.

"Well, it is tiny and cold to boot. I think the rats and mice sleep there too. I am not even sure I will fit laying down flat." Quinn tried to downplay his success.

"Do you want to play dice with us?" The boys liked Quinn to be in charge of the game to keep the peace.

"Tomorrow night, I promise. The doctor gave me a job and I want to finish it as soon as possible." He waved to his friends and headed to the galley to prepare to work on his new project. He wanted to please the doctor who reminded him of his father. The man had a meticulous and confident personality, yet had a kind eye. He felt the need to impress Pixie as well. Perhaps being a whaler would be alright after all. Having permission to keep an oil lamp, he worked late into the evening.

CHAPTER 6

Making an Iron Harpoon

Quinn settled into his job in the galley. Although technically he reported to the Chef, his skills soon placed him in the position of carpenter. He found himself in charge of maintaining many items on the ship - from cutlery, handles, and whaling equipment to the doctors' surgical tools. One morning he was drawn to the top deck due to the crew shouting and cheering.

"What's going on?" he asked the gathering group of whalers.

"The chase boats are next to the ship." An onlooker stepped aside so Quinn could get to step close to the railing.

Looking to the water, he was surprised to see both the hunting craft and the whale in question so close to the vessel. Generally the action took place much further off in the distance. Once the whales were sighted, the chase boats were lowered to the water and sailed off in pursuit. He had heard stories of crews getting lost and never finding their way back to the ship. The sail on the chase boat had been stowed and the men were furiously rowing after the whale. Quinn could not help but get caught up in the excitement of the hunt for the first time.

Although being in the chase craft entailed the most danger of injury or death to a crewmember, there were many who coveted being part of the team. The harpooner or boat steerer stood in the front and was a strong and proud man. They tended to be aloof to the rest of the crew. Other than the Captain and the mates, they were the most admired and respected. Very skillful at serving death, they had more ferocity than a basic executioner. Every time a harpoon is thrown, different angles and depths are at play. He had to be agile and fast thinking and was the life blood of the ship. The mate or officer was at the stern working the tiller.

The whale had turned back towards the mother ship and Quinn could see that one iron had already caused a gash but was no longer attached. But the animal was wounded and the chase crew was able to come beside the whale and launch a second iron which met its mark and wedged deep into the side of the leviathan. Quinn watched as the whale exhaled, its breath tinged with red. It tried in vain to dive into the water but the weight of the boat held tight against the ropes. Surfacing again, the magnificent creature rolled onto its side as the waters around it turned dark with blood. The mate then came forward to the bow, changing places with the boat steerer and delivered the killing blow.

A hoorah erupted from the side as the larger whaling vessel as the crew yelled "there she blows." That was the chant for when whales were sighted, or during the chase when the lungs were pierced and the battle for the chase crew was won. Quinn felt pride for the men and sorrow for the whale. Seeing the life force slowly leave the animal, he had to turn away from the scene. He slipped into the throngs behind him who quickly took his spot at the edge.

Later in the day the irons were brought to him for evaluation and refining. He turned the metal over and over in his hands. This particular harpoon had come loose from the whale during the hunt. Studying the integrity of the metal he felt the sharpness of the point and sides. Its only fault was that it failed to fully pierce the blubber. Once penetrated through the skin , the spear needed to rotate slightly to be seated. Otherwise it could come back as soon as force was applied.

His thoughts went back to his father with a touch of sadness. He envisioned working with the shoe leather back at home. They had an instrument that once it pierced into the leather, a hinge swung out and effectively held the hide until released. His mind churned over the similarities and an idea began to take form and he headed for the smithy.

"I have an idea for an iron. Is there some extra metal that we could experiment with?" Quinn worked closely with the blacksmith and they had become friends of sorts.

"What would you like to me do?" The older man flashed him a grin showing his missing teeth.

Quinn prepared to explain his revolutionary idea. It was unlike the flared point he held in his hand. "I want the blade to start with a narrow point, then flare out in the body but curve up and back down to the shaft."

"But what holds the point in the whale. You have to have wings of some sort?" Smithy looked perplexed.

"I want to attach a bar here on the side that swings. When the iron pierces past the length of the bar and is pulled backwards, the hinge will swing down and act as an anchor. As long as the pin holds, the harpoon is secure." Quinn looked at the Smithy who was silent for a few minutes.

With a shrug, Smithy started to pound the metal. It was unlike any design he had ever been asked to assemble. Thinking the young man was quite daft, he never the less worked on the project. Over the days, Quinn would work with each prototype, moving back the hinge, making the swing longer or shorter. He experimented with the shape, creating a larger curve on the top of the blade than the bottom. Finally, one day Quinn held up the new iron and proclaimed it was done. Holding it above his arm and plunging the shaft into a burlap sack of material, the point could not be extricated.

Smithy's approving eyes met Quinn's with a smile. "Sonny, I think you are on to something. This may actually work. I wonder if we can get any of the harpooners to give it a try. They are a superstitious lot and very set in their ways. Guess we could approach the Captain or even one of the mates."

"First I'll show Chef and he can advise us how to proceed." Quinn had kept his invention a secret just in case the idea was a failure. Barely able to contain his excitement, he left the blacksmith at a trot to show Pixie the new tool.

Protecting the new iron under his arm, Quinn cursed as the ship bounced in rough seas. As the ship cut through a large wave, water spilled over the gunwale and onto the gangway as the boat was buffeted sideways. Quinn's footing slipped and he slammed into a set of crates and fell to the deck. A sharp pain in the lower left abdomen cruelly reminded him that he had the metal against his side. His mind tried to process the injury as crewmembers rushed to his aid.

A voice gasped in surprise. "Why is there blood on the deck?"

Quinn rolled over and realized his shirt was staining red. "I had a blade in my hand. I must have cut myself with it when I slipped." He looked around the ground in concern. "There it is, by that crate. Please grab it for me."

Helping the wounded sailor to his feet, the man assisted him to the infirmary. "Doc, Quinn has stabbed himself in the side with this. He is bleeding pretty good." The sailor helped Quinn to the table and handed the strangely shaped blade to the doctor.

The doctor immediately started to arrange cleansing alcohol and instruments onto a tray. "Help him remove his shirt and lay him on his back please." Taking the strange iron closer to the light, he studied the unusual shape. Expecting the blade to be symmetrical on the top and the bottom, it appeared to have a part missing. Concern quickened his pulse as whalers had died over the years from blood poisoning. "Here Quinn, take a bit of rum. I'm afraid this is going to hurt a bit." The doctor cleaned the injury with the astringent and used retractors to spread the wound. Quinn squeezed his eyes shut and groaned as the doctor probed deeply.

"For goodness sake's boy, how did you manage to stab yourself? I cannot find the other piece of metal."

"Why do you think there is metal in my wound?" Quinn was beginning to crave another glass of rum.

"The tip that was in your hand was broken. The bottom half must have sheared off." The doctor leaned over to the desk and grabbed the tool.

"Let me see it." The doctor brought over the iron and Quinn started to laugh and shake his head. "Doc, you can quit torturing me. There is nothing missing. I made a new type of harpoon point."

"What type of harpoon point?" a new voice commanded from the doorway. Avery, the first mate of the ship had been sent by the Captain to discover who had been injured and to what extent. He came closer and picked up the iron. Turning the device back and forth in his hands, he intently studied the hinge mechanism and admired the sharpness of the edge. "Explain yourself, sailor." Although Avery was fairly young, he was used to seniority.

"I have been working on a new idea for a few weeks. I made an iron that will stay secure as long as the hinge engages. I fell on it when the ship turned sideways in the wave." Quinn's voice quivered with embarrassment and fear. He had been working on his invention without the officer's knowledge or permission. To have slipped on deck and wounded himself with it only added insult to the injury.

Avery looked questioningly at the doctor. "What is the damage, doctor?"

"The wound is significant but did not penetrate into the abdomen. As long as it does not get infected he should be fine." The doctor turned away, knowing full well that even simple cuts could fester and turn deadly. He had few medicines available on the boat and sometimes healing seemed more up to fate than his skill. Taking a needle and thread, he began to suture the skin back together.

Avery turned to leave and wrapped the harpoon in some cloth. "I am going to take this with me for now. Good job, Doctor." He raised his eyebrows at Quinn but did not address him further.

"Okay, that should do it. Have a small drink with me before you go. Other than enduring the taunts of the crew, I believe you will be fine." The doctor poured two small glasses with his rum. He liked his red-haired assistant. He did excellent work with the tools and was smart. They had begun to have some interesting philosophical conversations when Quinn brought the midday meal to his office.

"Do you think I'll be punished? I took it upon myself to make the tool." Quinn began to worry. This was not the way he had intended to present his invention.

"Avery looked more intrigued than angry. He may reprimand you but I don't think so." The man put back on his spectacles and waved Quinn off with a smile as he started to write in his log. "Bandage yourself and keep it changed daily."

Several days later, Quinn was summoned to the top gangway. First mate Avery, the Captain, and the harpooners were waiting for him. The hunters leaned casually against some timbers with their arms folded across their chests. Their demeanors were mostly aloof but slightly vexed at the same time. They clearly did not appreciate their time being wasted.

"Quinn, I have been studying your design. I find it quite revolutionary. Can you give us a demonstration?" the Captain asked, as he handed him the iron.

"Yes, let me grab a shaft in my shop." Quinn quickly returned and secured the harpoon to a piece of wood. "As long as the blade is inserted past the hinge, the iron will stay secure. When pulled backwards, the arm acts as an anchor." With a trembling hand and a quick prayer, he thrust the spear into stacked burlap he had brought along. "Now it should be stuck." He pulled backwards onto the shaft which did not budge from the cloth.

A senior harpooner named Charles strode forward to the spear, meeting Quinn's eyes with a steely stare. He placed his feet on either side of the bags and yanked backwards. Quinn gulped as the sinewy muscles in his back flexed. Using his knife, he freed the harpoon for evaluation. He shook his head as he turned it back and forth in his hand. "Okay, I will give it a try." He glanced at Avery, who was the mate in charge of his chase boat. Clearly the officer wanted to experiment with it. "I hope we don't lose too many whales." He spoke directly to Quinn but a hint of a smile curved the corners of his mouth.

Realizing that his shoulders were starting to ache, Quinn let out a huge sigh of relief. Walking back to the galley, he touched his healing injury in appreciation. The officers looked pleased with the performance of the harpoon although the true test would be in the ocean. He felt confident that piece of metal would change his fate.

CHAPTER 7

Jonas

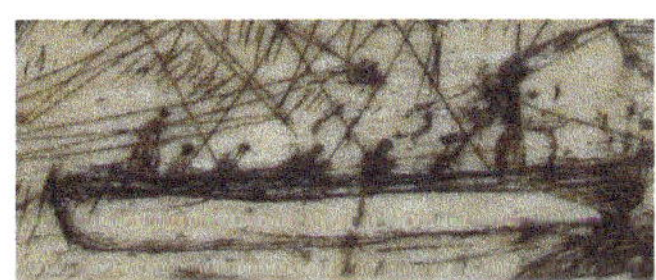

The following weeks, Charles the harpooner experimented with the new apparatus. He called on Quinn to make small changes and discuss angles and technique. The young man found his status had risen and he felt new respect from the crew. Charles and his mates were adored, and with Quinn in their inner circle he also garnered new attention.

Quinn stopped by the area where chase crews congregated to drop off newly repaired equipment. Charles was high in the mast, as two men, either boat steerers or mates, usually scanned the horizon for whales. If the animals were sighted, they controlled the direction of the ship over the Captain. Jonas stood up and they slapped hands. The young man had been working in the chase boat for the past several weeks. The feisty nature required to be on the crew fit him perfectly. Although their jobs had different responsibilities, their days in the hold had sealed their bond as close friends. He was putting Flemish coiling ropes into a large bucket for the upcoming hunting excursion when he motioned Quinn to sit next to him.

"Do you like being part of the chase crew?" Quinn asked him. Although Quinn was glad his job entailed him staying on board, he still held admiration for the strength required to navigate the small boats.

"Well, I row like hell until my muscles ache but I am getting stronger. The ride is truly exciting and sometimes I think the boat is going to be knocked upside down. There is definitely a perk being associated with these gents as they eat a heck of a lot better than we used too. Hmm, better rum too. What's up with that?" Jonas cocked his head sideways in question.

"Chef's secret. See you tonight for dice?" Quinn called as he returned to his shop.

"Absolutely." Jonas flashed a grin in his direction.

Later that morning, a man ran through the doorway out of breath. "Quinn! Come right now. The doc wants you in his office immediately."

"What wrong? Did somebody get hurt?" Quinn dropped his tools and immediately strode after the other whaler.

"One of the chase boats got stoved by a whale. There are some injuries."

They arrived at the infirmary and Quinn was surprised to find Charles standing just inside the room looking ashen. "I'm so sorry. The whale came up under the bow of the boat and the tail pushed us upwards. I had the harpoon ready but the force threw us up into the air. Jonas was underneath me when we landed."

Fear surged in Quinn's heart as he saw rare emotion in the harpooners' eyes. Hurrying into the room, he recoiled at the amount of blood that covered the table where his friend Jonas lay under the doctor's care. The injured man was breathing quickly and was in obvious agony.

"Quinn, the harpoon has engaged the hinge and I cannot get it out." The doctor's voice calmly commanded him to think. A broken shaft protruded from Jonas' side, the iron hidden beneath the skin's surface. Blood seeped from the wound while the doctor held a dressing in place to staunch the flow. A pile of red soaked cloth was already on the floor. "Can you tell me how to remove it?"

With his pulse pounding in his ears, Quinn struggled to think. "We have to dismantle the hinge. Let me get some tools."

Dashing from the room, he ran across the hallway and up the stairs to gather the equipment from his workshop. The crew had started to congregate around the doctors' room and he cried at them to stand aside. Back at the surgical table, he grimaced as the doctor spread the wound. Blood seeped outwards, obscuring his view. With trembling hands, Quinn meticulously disengaged the hinge from the blade, alternating with the doctor who would re-apply pressure to the gushing wound. Finally with the pin removed, the harpoon point was extricated. The doctor quickly went to work trying to stop the bleeding.

Quinn took Jonas' hand in his and stood at his side. Their eyes locked and Quinn offered words of encouragement. The young man smiled back and his head rolled to the side. Quinn's skin prickled as a shiver caressed his entire body. "Doctor, I think he's gone," he whispered.

The doctor stopped probing to glance at Jonas. Placing his ear to his chest, he nodded his head in agreement. "He lost too much blood. I could not save him. I know he was your friend. I am truly sorry."

Quinn backed up until he bumped into the cabinet, sinking down to the floor and burst into tears. "Oh my god, I killed him. My harpoon killed him." He covered his face with his hands as unbidden tears streamed down his cheeks.

The doctor wiped his hands and came over to Quinn. Leaning down to the floor he offered him a clean linen. Quinn looked at him, emotional pain radiating from his eyes. Handing him the cloth, the doctor put his hands on the young man's shoulders and said, "Please, call me William."

CHAPTER 8

The Baby Whale

Quinn felt numb for days. On a whaling vessel, accidents happened routinely, some of which resulted in death. He had been assisting the doctor for months and was well-aware of this. However, losing his friend left him depressed.

"You did a nice reading for Jonas. I really appreciate that." Quinn and the doctor sat together in his office and the young man mused as the older man ate but they shared a small glass of rum. The doctor not only mended souls, but acted as chaplain to usher them to the afterlife. "What happens after we die?"

"Well, there are many explanations in the Bible. I do believe there is something more. There is a life force in everything around us. I cannot believe that it simply ceases to exist. Perhaps it just changes from its current form." The doctor had been worried for his friend. He had seen men spiral into the depths of despair before. Quinn had stood silent and disconnected as they lowered Jonas into the sea while he read chosen verses from his book. The memorial was simple and quick. The Captain actually preferred no ceremony take place at all as he felt it might undermine his authority. All Captains secretly worried about their crew placing blame on the command.

"I saw an angel once, back in the hold when George passed. She was beautiful." Quinn closed his eyes and replayed the visage. Her golden outline was stamped in his memory. "Do you think she came for Jonas?" Quinn whispered the secret he had not divulged to any other soul.

William noted the dark circles under his friend's eyes, supporting the fact that he was not sleeping. Was he hallucinating now as well? "You cannot feel responsible for Jonas. Any iron would have caused a similar injury. You know that. It was not your fault the whale tossed the chase crew."

"I understand that." Quinn grappled with his guilt. "But I cannot help thinking if I could have taken the hinge apart sooner, or better yet, never made the darn thing in the first place. Perhaps the outcome would have been different."

"What's done is done and can't be changed. I am not even sure there is a lesson to be learned. Perhaps that is why people believe in God. We need to give purpose to events. To relieve our consciousness in what part we may have played."

"Why are you here on the vessel and not practicing in town? You are clearly an excellent physician." Quinn asked this question, feeling their relationship was strong enough to hear the answer.

"I used to be a very heavy drinker and made a medical mistake. Perhaps it was God's will that I ended up here. See, I just justified my existence." He shook his head and smiled at his own humor. "Anyways, I know the guilt of feeling responsible. The Captain gave me this opportunity to continue as a medical professional."

Quinn smiled at his friend. "Thank you William for our talks. I had better get back."

Several days later while at his work bench, Quinn felt a shiver pass through his body and the hairs on his arms stood upright. He had this same emotion twice before. First at George's passing, and just recently with the death of Jonas. He stopped working and looked around the room. Voices were raised and there was commotion on the processing deck. Going out to investigate, he stopped abruptly in his tracks as he came around the corner. Before him was an infant whale that had slipped from the birth canal of the now deceased mother during the processing. It lay prone on the deck, the block and tackle still secured around its tail as it was just hauled from the waters below. Membranes still draped over its body but it was still alive. The men stood in a circle and looked at one another with uncertainty. One of the mates came forward with a spear and plunged it deep into its chest. The kill was reserved for the upper echelon of command. The baby seemed to look straight at Quinn as its eye went blank. The mother whale had been taken with one harpoon. His creation had performed its job with deadly accuracy he thought as he stumbled from the processing deck and around the corner. He felt like an accomplice to murder.

"Quinn, I did not realize she was pregnant or I would have never chosen her. " Charles had spied Quinn start to leave the deck and followed behind him. "I never take a whale if I see a youngster at her side."

Quinn stopped to face the man. "Honestly, I cannot explain it. But sometimes I can feel their death." He squeezed his eyes shut and rubbed his hand hard over his face. "I wish I were not like this. I don't know if I can take it anymore. I feel like my harpoon is an instrument of evil."

Although Charles liked the man in front of him, he had diffi- culty sympathizing with his emotions. He and Quinn were simply cut from different cloth. "We had to put the baby out of its misery. It would have never survived." Not knowing what else to say, he shrugged and walked back to the deck.

Quinn turned to look at the whales one last time. A rivulet of partially congealed blood ran down the board towards his shoe. Leaning down, he scooped some in his hand and returned to the galley. Taking a small glass container, he placed the mixture high onto a shelf.

"Quinn can you get me some rum from storage?" Chef was busy preparing the officers' meal. When the young man did not answer, he turned around and looked at the frail form behind him. "What is wrong? You look terrible." The chef frowned. Ever since Jonas's death, Quinn had become more and more melanchol- ic. Perhaps the doctor could talk some sense into him, he mused.

"Take this plate to the Doc and see if he needs anything repaired."

William was organizing his shelf when Quinn arrived. "Ahh, thank you my boy, I was getting hungry." Glancing over, he noted the sunken cheekbones which were showing under the red beard. "You are looking thinner, did you eat today?"

"I just don't have an appetite." Quinn waved off the bread offered by the doctor. "I watched them kill the baby whale on deck today and felt sick afterwards. I was never meant to be a whaler, I am sure of that."

The man sat back in his chair, and removed his spectacles. "Who is to say what our destiny is, or what we do with it. You are unusual in the depth of your heart. Too bad you did not go to medical school as I suspect you would have been a great doctor. All of us experience loss. Many times I am left to make sense on how one man can survive a catastrophic injury, yet another dies with a small cut. I can only do my best and accept the outcome." He sighed and took a fresh sip of rum as he reminisced. "I also lost my will when I could no longer practice medicine in town. But here I am, being a doctor, making a difference, and surrounded by good people. Sometimes you have to dig deep and find purpose inside yourself or you will wither away."

"I know, William. I will try." Quinn left the doctor's room and ascended the steps to the aft deck and made his way to the side wall. Leaning his elbows on the top rail, he briefly closed his eyes and listened to the waves caress the hull of the boat. If a man fell overboard, they were rarely retrieved. To stop the forward motion of a vessel of this magnitude, turn around and get back to the original spot was incredibly difficult. Even lowering a chase boat took time. It would not take much to fall over into the water. He studied the turbulent wake created by the boat's passage as it smoothed out to become congruent with the sea and the heart of the ocean seemed to beckon him.

Contemplating whether he was capable of such an act, a fluttering noise drew his attention. Quinn was shocked to see a hummingbird just feet away from him, its wings vibrating so fast that they were a blur. Mesmerized, he looked around. They were far from land and he had never heard of a hummingbird at sea. The small creature landed on the wood railing nearby and appeared to evaluate him as it cocked its small head side to side. Radiant colors glowed from its' crown in the sunlight as the bird stared eye to eye with Quinn. Then with a flash, it took wing and was gone.

Wonder and awe filled him. How was the bird this far out? It was as if the animal had looked directly into his soul. He found himself scanning the sky but the creature was nowhere to be seen. He stepped away from the rail and sat heavily onto a crate. This was the second time he had contemplated taking his own life. Quinn found himself thinking of his father and could imagine the disapproval. Walking back to the galley, he acknowledged that although this is not the life he would have chosen, he would perform it to the best of his ability. He would play the cards he had been dealt.

The Chair

The ship was moving at a good clip when one of the sails separated from the rigging. Orders were made to stop forward motion and evaluate the damage. The bosun called for Quinn and his tools. "Quinn, I need you to go on the chair and mend the sail." The man opened and closed his injured hand as he contemplated if he could do the job himself but his fingers would barely move. "I have already shown you how to make repairs, only you will be high in the air. Are you afraid of heights?"

"Uh, I don't know sir. I don't think so." Quinn looked dubiously at the boatswain chair. Securing his satchel of tools around his shoulder, he sat onto the small wooden board and grabbed onto the ropes. As the men worked the pulley, Quinn found himself bobbing forward and backwards as he struggled to maintain his balance. Upon reaching the broken sail, he looked down to the deck. After a moment of vertigo, he felt an elation of freedom never felt before. The ebb and flow of the tides was amplified at this height and he was oddly comforted. At this elevation the surface of the ocean had different contours and colors.

"You are supposed to fix the sail while you are up there, not gawk." The bosun yelled upwards when it became clear that his pupil had become distracted.

Quinn finished the repair and waved that he was ready to come down. The older man helped him from the chair and steadied him as he got his feet back on the deck. "How did you do? Any problems?"

"At first I was a bit nervous but then it was fine. In fact, I kind of liked being up there." Quinn was exhilarated. Some days at sea could be quite monotonous and this certainly helped break up the routine.

"Well that's just fine. You see, until my hand heals, you can help with some of the repairs I need done. Make sure it does not interfere with your other duties." The older man wanted to make sure to keep the peace with Pixie and the doctor.

The next day, Quinn was sent over the side of the ship. Dangling precariously close to the swells, he found this position much more disconcerting. Hearing laughing above, suddenly the chair dipped straight into the ocean. Cold water soaked his pants and threatened to climb into his shirt as he yelled out loud. The current quickly swept him backwards and towards the hull when the chair yanked back into the air. Grasping onto the ropes, he cursed as some of his supplies sank into the ocean. His anger quickly simmered when he was pulled to the deck where several of the older sailors were doubled over in mirth. Everybody quickly settled as officer Avery came around the corner.

"What's going on here?" The mate had been drawn over by the laughing. His tone was sharp and commanding.

"Just showing Quinn the art of the chair," one of the sailors mumbled.

Avery was not amused. Playing jokes on each other showed a lack of discipline and an injury could always follow. "Go dry off before you take ill," he growled to Quinn. "And you," addressing the bosun's crew, "no rum for you tonight." He turned sharply to leave.

The sailor pounded on Quinn's shoulder with his good hand after the officer had departed. "That's okay, it was worth it. By the way, you scream a bit like a girl." All the men laughed again in unison and Quinn thinly smiled.

"What happened to you?" Pixie wryly asked as water dripped from Quinn's pants. He had returned to his bunk to dry off.

"A rite of passage I think," he replied as he rummaged through his belongings for dry clothing.

"I suspect it's a matter of time before they have you pulling more weight." Pixie was actually pleased since Quinn had been in better spirits the past few weeks. Working the chair was to become part of the lineage of the boat and carried with it position and pride. "But I still need you during the day."

"Please make sure you do. You, the doc, and this part of the ship are like my home. I am comfortable here." Quinn quickly changed and began helping store the pans. "I hear we are headed back to home port in a few months. I can't believe we have been at sea for over two years. Do you think I will be allowed to go ashore?"

"Possibly, if the Captain can be assured you won't try to run off. William and I will see what we can do."

That evening, Quinn retired to his bed and calmed himself by whittling a piece of wood. He had taken to making figurines of sea creatures and mermaids. At first they were crude replicas but he had improved in his sophistication. Even the old sailor Isaac had commented on a few of his molds. What Quinn really wanted was a journal but there was very little free paper on the boat. Even reading material was at a minimum. Other than the Sailors Physician and other medical text in William's office, or manuals on how to make soap, no stories or books were at his disposal. Would he be able to go ashore when they arrived in harbor? What would he say to his family? Would he try to run even though he would promise the Captain he would not? Finally, sleep overtook him and he dreamed uneasily of snow lit streets.

Home Port

The months passed and the whaler slipped into the New Bedford port. The Captain commanded the ship's bell be rung as the men started to dismantle the large whale oil cooking kettles or the try-works. Taking bricks that had deteriorated over the long voyage, they tossed them overboard into the ocean.

"Quinn, the Captain has given permission for you to help Doc get supplies later in the week after unloading. We have assured him that you are trustworthy. You know our reputations have been put at stake for you." Pixie shook a finger at him. Many of the crew would legally disembark never to be seen again. Between desertions at sea, and sailors leaving at the end of a trip, each voyage could have an entirely new set of personnel. However, the whaling companies were quite clever at keeping a good proportion of their subjects in bondage.

"I know, I will make it up to you. I need to see my father and my brother. I just disappeared and they never knew what happened." Quinn figured he would not have much time to himself but he was sure he could fit in a quick reunion.

"Don't take anything with you except the clothes on your back. That will make the officers nervous."

Barrels of oil soon choked the waters around the wharf as the ship offloaded its cargo. Sperm whale oil was stored separately from all other whale oil, and the Captain smiled at the specially marked casks. Bone and other products harvested from the whales were carried on the backs of men and placed into skiffs.

When the holds were emptied, the ship sighed in relief and bobbed much higher in the water. Quinn was finally given the nod of consent to join the doctor's landing party. The short ride in the chase boat seemed to take hours. Stepping out of the boat and onto the dock, Quinn realized he was still moving with the ocean which made him queasy.

"Wow, I am not feeling well." Although they had stopped at many ports the past few years, Quinn had always been relegated to stay in the boat.

"Don't worry, it will pass," the doctor assured him. "Which way to your father's shop?"

Quinn pointed further into the middle of town and he found himself becoming increasingly nervous as they approached the street where his family's store resided.

"Wait! Where is it?" Quinn whirled in confusion. They were in front of the storefront where his father's business was, but the sign was different. Dashing through the door, he approached the owner. "What happened to the cobbler that used to be here?"

"I have been here for at least a year. I believe the tenant before me caught ill and died. His wife moved back north I think." The man cleaned some glassware on his apron to arrange on the shelf where the shoes had once been displayed.

Quinn was shocked. His mind panicked at the thought of his father's death. That was not a scenario he had expected. "What about his son, he was about my age, with light red hair?"

"I did not know the family personally. I am sorry. Are you related to them?" He could see the distress on the young man's face when he shook his head yes. "Perhaps you can find your mother up north?"

"She was my father's second wife. Our mother passed away when we were younger." Quinn thanked him and exited the building with the doctor.

"I'm sorry, Quinn. Did you have an uncle or other family in town?" The doctor tried to be helpful although he knew they did not have time to mount a citywide search.

"No, it was just us." He looked around the street as people brushed past them and he felt estranged. There was no telling where his younger brother may have gone too. The boy was adventurous and if their father was dead, he most likely headed west. Unfolding the Chef's list from his pocket, he said, "Let's get our supplies so we can get back to the ship," and they headed back down towards the docks.

CHAPTER 11

The Storm

he two men walked in silence down the bustling street. Quinn was deep in thought and the doctor seemed a bit edgy.

William suddenly stopped and put his hand to Quinn's shoulder. "I know this was unexpected and believe me, I feel for you." He glanced up a side street. "I need to see some people but you need to get to the dock to check Pixie's supplies. I'll meet you there so wait for me before going back to the ship. You'll be there - right? You are not about to run off in despair or anything?" His eyebrows arched high onto his forehead to accentuate the question.

"Yea – I'll be there. I don't really have anywhere else to go." Quinn rubbed the facial hair that was growing on his chin. He had not decided if he wanted to keep a beard or a clean face. With a shrug, they parted company.

Quinn was busy checking boxes and barrels against the list when the doctor arrived and glanced over into the boat that was being loaded. "We have a few more goods coming. Ahh – there they are."

A wagon pulled onto the dock and the driver handed Quinn a board to initial. "Make sure they stay standing upwards and be careful with them," as he motioned to the new containers that were being unloaded onto the planks by his men.

Quinn signed the paper and noted the contents as DELIVER TO GALLEY. Hmm, this must be the special supplies the Chef had told him about. He directed them to a safe place on the skiff and they all stepped aboard and disembarked for the ship. "Do you know where we are headed? Sure seems like quite a bit of supplies." Quinn had made a mental count of the number of journeys the small boat made back and forth.

"I believe we are in for a trip around the Horn." The doctor wiped his forehead with a fine handkerchief. "That's the tip of South America if you didn't know. It's been a while since I have been on that route."

They reached the side of the ship and began the process of bringing the goods aboard. The doctor instructed one of the hands to take his particular boxes to the infirmary. "Put this in the corner of my office, and Quinn, you personally take the Chef his items. I would hate to see any precious rum or other supplies disappear." With a wink of his eye, he turned on his heel and strode off down the deck.

Quinn levered the large barrel labeled GALLEY and went to the kitchen. "Gees, Pixie, what do you have in here?" he asked through labored breaths as he placed the container where the cook had gestured with his good thumb. His other thumb was subject to an unfortunate accident caused by too much drink and rough seas. Pixie liked to chop quickly and efficiently and was quite surprised when a jolt of pain registered in his pleasantly dulled mind. "Oh crap," he thought when he looked down to see his fingernail and some finger attached had joined the potatoes. William had stared in disbelief when Pixie had delivered the dismembered digit to the doctor.

"Just what do you want me to do with that?" The doctor looked into his own palm where the cook had just dropped the lonely appendage.

"Well, I was thinking you could put it back on." The man held up his hastily wrapped hand with the blood soaking through the bandage.

"Yes, I will fix this." William stood from his chair and walked over to the window which was slightly ajar and tossed it into the sea. "Okay, let me look at the rest." He removed the bandage and closed the skin over the remaining finger the best he could.

Back in the galley, the Chef had his back to Quinn and seemed quite pleased. "How did the meeting go with the family?"

"They were gone. Father is dead, my stepmother moved back north, and my brother is missing."

"Ahh, damn. I'm sorry about that." The burly man stopped cooking and wiped his hands. Going over to the barrel of special rum, he poured two small casks. "Here's to you Quinn. You truly are part of our family now."

The next several weeks entailed outfitting the vessel for her new voyage. The hull was re-caulked and the try works cooking apparatus which held the large cooking vats was reconfigured. The goose pen - a box which held water underneath the fires, keeping the deck from getting too hot and burning - was removed of rotting wood. A secondary goose pen in the deck directly below was checked for leaks. A triangular hole in the gangway allowed rapid filling of the usually dry container. Rollo loved to tell stories of the try pot falling through the weakened wood to the bottom of the ship. Fire onboard could easily spell disaster for the entire crew.

Quinn was allowed into town to assist with the refitting. A few visits with old acquaintances confirmed his fear that his brother was not around. Owning nothing of value and having no money, he had no choice but to call the ship home and the crew his family. Finally the Captain gave the order to leave port and head southward into the Atlantic.

Water sprayed onto the decks as the whaler cut through white capped waves. The crew had been underway for weeks, veering off course to hunt if the opportunity presented itself. However, rough seas and a cloudy sky made spotting the spouts of whales quite difficult. As they approached southern waters, the chase boats were tightly secured and the sails reefed as the fabric snapped back and forth in gale-type winds.

The ship lurched to the side as Quinn braced himself next to the wall in the galley. "Bloody hell, these seas are horrendous. I know you said the weather can be unpredictable, but this is reminding me of my days in the hold. " He grimaced as a wave of queasiness washed over him. He was not the only sailor to be experiencing anxiety and nausea and some of the newest recruits were having a particularly hard time.

Chef looked pensively out the galley door towards the dark clouds that seemed to be encircling them from all sides. Tenderly caressing the wood of the wall, he closed his eyes. "She will get us there in one piece. You just have to love and trust her."

Both men stood at attention as the Captain stepped into the galley. His silver eyebrows knit together with concern and small drops of rain water glistened from his beard. "I am afraid we are going to catch this storm after all. We will eat early tonight, a short simple meal even for the officers. Secure everything except what you need."

With a curt nod, the Captain left and started barking orders to his subordinates. Men were busy rearranging sail and rope as decisions were made for direction and speed. They had tried to outrun the storm but it was too massive and they would soon be in its jaws. Quinn doubled-checked that all knifes were secure in their scabbards and the barrels of supplies were tied down. He excused himself as he went to the infirmary to deliver the doctor's meal and some repaired tools.

"Would you please close my window?" the doctor asked as Quinn entered his chambers. Quinn secured the round porthole that was cracked open ever so gently to relieve the smell of the rubbing alcohols. "So it appears we are to enter God's wrath." The doctor seemed resigned to the challenge. "Have you made the arrangements to catch the rain?"

Quinn shrugged and tried to see the benefits of the upcoming storm. He had prepared all the fresh water riggings earlier with a special device on the masts which gathered and ferried rainwater to waiting barrels below. Nothing made tempers run short like water rationing. "Yes I have, William," he said softly. Quinn and the doctor had become the most unlikely of friends, even to the point of sharing meals at lunch. Never would an officer and enlisted man be able to sit together to dine, but they ate in the privacy of Doc's room. "I'll be on deck working the ropes along with most of the other men. Isn't it ironic how we all would rather be washed to sea than be caught under the deck in a sinking ship?"

"I may need to call on you if we have any injuries. Please make sure you lash yourself in properly." The older man worried briefly. He had known the Captain for some years and could accurately read the weathered man's emotions. He had seen the look in his piercing eyes. Like an animal cornered with its back to the wall, ready to give fight.

Soon they were cloaked in darkness as the boat succumbed to the brunt of the storm. Rain and wind tossed the crew mercilessly in the dark void that had become the ocean. Even Quinn's heavily oiled jacket and hood could not keep the water from soaking his skin as waves crashed over the bow and threatened to scour the deck clean. Although he tried to manage the fresh water barrels, he found himself hugging a heavy piling for most of the time. Exhausted and cold, he focused on the sound of the wood creaking as the bow broke water and the distant shouts in the background as those in charge of the wheel shouted directions.

"Wave ahead. Hold fast," yelled the front watchman as he frantically rung the ship's bell.

A massive wall of water advanced into view as the helmsman frantically spun the wheel. As the boat began to climb upwards, Quinn felt his feet drop out from under him and he fell to his knees. The ropes bit into his wrists as he was partially suspended from his ties. The ship almost pointed vertical as she crested the top of the wave. Hovering near the top, Quinn wondered if they might travel to the stars as the craft balanced ever so precariously and seemed to consider her options for just a moment before plunging down the other side. All the whalers slid forward and grabbed on for dear life as the ship quickly gained velocity and rocketed downwards. Once in the trough, the bow buried deep in the base of the next wave, not unlike casting a spear into the great whale herself. A cascade of water drenched the entire deck. Men lost their grip, lashings snapped, and wood could be heard cracking all around. Barrels, sail, pieces of masts, and men slid helplessly along the slick surface and over the edge.

Quinn held his breath and closed his eyes. Water pummeled his body and one arm loosened but his ropes held him in place. The same hemp binds which held him hostage now kept his life from being flung to the sea. Feeling incredulous that he survived, the moment of elation was quickly quelled. Men and supplies were being washed overboard. Untying himself, he ran to the edge to assist those still hanging on. Some faces in the water quickly drifted from sight and were gone forever.

The triage had begun. Quinn gathered a prone man under his shoulder and headed for the doctor's office. Men continued to arrive with lacerations and broken bones. Flying wood projectiles caused grim injuries and the doctor was busy binding wounds and performing amputations. Quinn knew the equipment and procedures as well as any medical personal. The floor became slippery with blood as the two worked on continuously. A commotion in the hallway interrupted their concentration as a man was helped hobble into the room. The doctor swore under his breath as he recognized the pale face of his Captain.

"Clear a table and get my retractor," the doctor boomed as he spied a slow lava of red seeping from the man's lower leg. Slicing up the seam of the pants, William exposed the blood-soaked limb. Wooden shards and the metal binding of a barrel entwined itself with the muscle of the Master's calf. "Get some drink for the Captain!"

Quinn poured rum into a tumbler but the old-time sailor waved it off. "Do what you need to, doctor. Save our precious drink for celebrations together."

Placing a spreader to expose the gash, William's heart thumped in his chest. My god, he had not felt this nervous in years. He almost considered taking the rum for himself. The wood was splintered but more concerning was the rusty metal which peppered the injury. Blood constantly obstructed his view as a substantial vessel had been nicked in the process. Sweat moistened his glasses as he removed every visible remnant of debris.

Convinced he could do more, the doctor wrapped the leg and finally the Captain took the drink and glanced at one of the mates standing in the corner. "How many have we lost?"

"Two have perished from trauma so far and I believe the count is six men over the side. Three were retrieved." One of the officers sent by Avery to check on the Captain who was watching silently from the shadows stepped into view.

The Captain nodded in acknowledgment. "How bad is it, doctor?" he motioned to the leg.

"I believe I can save the leg, Eligh. You lost some of the blood supply and cut half your muscles, but as long as your foot does not swell or turn color, we should be okay." The doctor turned to gather some of his dried coca leaves behind his desk. "Chew on these this morning and night for the pain. They will help you sleep. I need to change the bandages every day."

Quinn used a mop and bucket and cleaned the floors of the night's carnage. The morning light clawed itself onto the horizon and soon illuminated the residual storm clouds in brilliant purple and pink hues. The old adage of red skies in morning, sailors take warning held no such threat as the malevolent clouds receded, sated with their destruction. The doctor appeared exhausted and Quinn sensed cracks in his exterior.

How many times had Quinn felt despair, only to be rallied by his close friend. If it were not for the doctor, he would have hurled himself over the side of the railing long ago. Taking a tumbler from the cabinet, he filled the cup with rum and placed it into the man's hand. The doctor motioned to Quinn's cup and they raised their cups and drank in silence.

That morning, Quinn surveyed the damage. One of the masts had broken and some of the riggings had been torn from their attachments. The main sail could not be fully unfurled. Gathering a small explosive charge from one of the Powder Monkeys, he ascended in the chair to create a new pulley. With the wind blowing, he lit the charge and nothing happened. Damn, he cursed and peered into the cavity he had created. A small ember still burned and he quickly squeezed his lids shut and turned his face as the ordinate went off.

The shock of the explosion almost catapulted him from the narrow board. His cheek burned but he cautiously opened his eyes and was relieved to have vision. He knew his face was a mess but at least the chamber for the pulley was a success. Lowering himself to the deck, he sheepishly went to the doctor's office.

"Hey William, I had a small accident." Quinn covered his cheek with a blood-soaked cloth.

The doctor wiped the sleep from his eyes. "What the hell were you doing?" he asked as he clipped away the fledgling beard to get another look. "You burned yourself good. There will be a scar for sure. Better grow a thick beard or the men will think you are marked, being the superstitious ignorant bunch they are."

Full beard it is, Quinn decided before returning to work.

CHAPTER 12

The Turtles

The Captain gazed cautiously through his monocular at the ship's sail in the distance. His man high in the bosun chair had called down earlier, "There is a ship ahead to the south!" He unconsciously shifted his weight off his injured leg and inwardly groaned. His adored vessel and its crew had taken quite a beating in the last storm, the worst he remembered. But she had persevered and pushed onwards. He tried to take strength from her weathered wood, for he felt old and fragile. The injury on his leg refused to heal. The doctor had re-operated on the wound and searched for remnants but only pain and discomfort resulted from the exploration.

He watched the approaching boat, weighing options in his experienced mind. Pirates and even competitor whalers frequented the waters, ready to take advantage. He knew the men secretly coveted a pirates' life and the freedom which it supposedly entailed but meeting with a such a crew usually entailed loss of profit or death. He had learned how to barter with whale oil and politics and usually escaped relatively unscathed. But they needed supplies. They were down men and had suffered losses with the storm. Making a decision, he motioned to Quinn who sat high in the chair with his own looking glass to come down.

"What do you see?" The Captain relied on his staff's higher vantage point.

Quinn worked the ropes until he was in earshot of the deck. "She has a longer sloop than I have seen but I believe it is a whaling vessel. There are chase boats secured to the side. I don't recognize her flag. It's definitely not from Boston or any companies I recognize."

The Captain felt more secure in his decision. "Bring the flag down." He directed Quinn back up the mast to secure the flag in a show of good faith and put the armory on alert. When the opposing ship did the same, the two boats arced towards one another until they traveled parallel at a distance. Always studying each other, they slowly came closer and closer. The Captain made the decision to drops sails and the other vessel followed suit. The two crews warily assessed each other as ropes were tossed to the adjoining crew. Quinn's Captain chose to cross first. Using the top rope for balance, he ignored his injury as he scurried across the bottom rope to make greeting. Although any meeting at sea was potentially risky, the other ship did not show any sign of aggression.

Quinn studied the craft from his vantage point high in the area. He noted the beautiful lines and artfully crafted wood. The carved female angel that adorned the bow caught his attention and he briefly thought of the entity that had come for George from first days on the boat. He was relieved when tensions seemed to ease and more of the crew joined the other boat so he returned to the deck and the galley.

Chef arrived from speaking with Avery and approached Quinn. "Captain would like some of our best rum and some food to share at a meal. They are from Northern Europe and are not familiar with the eastern seaboard. Captain is going to exchange nautical charts for some of the supplies we lost during the storm."

Chef muttered to himself as he prepared his offering to share with the other crew and left for the other ship. A few hours later, he emerged from the other vessel and called to Quinn for help with the supplies. "Hey, buddy, I have a surprise for you." He grinned wickedly as strange accents greeted Quinn's ears.

Crew from the foreign ship struggled into the room with two large creatures. Even though he could not understand the words, he knew they were swearing. "What in tarnation are those?" Quinn was shocked to see an animal with a shell like a turtle but with fins instead of legs.

"These are turtles that live in the sea. They came from the waters off an island on the Pacific side of the America's. Captain traded maps in exchange for a bunch of supplies, and these." Pixie had clearly exchanged beverages with the other cook.

Quinn glanced at his new charges. They moved laboriously on fins, obviously an animal made for water. One of the sailors handed him a bag of seaweed and leafy plants and rattled off instructions that he could not understand before departing for their ship. Did they eat this for food? "How did the meal go?" he asked Pixie as he started to construct a makeshift pen.

"Great. As expected, my food was wonderful. Of course, nobody knew what the other person was saying, but my jokes were well-received."

They both laughed heartily as Quinn began ushering the animals into enclosure. He sat to study them. They had incredibly intelligent eyes. Deep limpid pools full of soul.

"Do they bite?"

"Nah, they're gentle as lambs," Chef responded as he watched with interest because he had no idea if they were aggressive or not. He had worked with land tortoise in the past, but never a sea turtle.

Quinn experimentally extended his hand and placed it on the head of the smaller turtle. Though the skin was cool, it was soft to the touch. He traced the white scar on its head, like the club marking on a card deck.

"Hello Club, how are you today?" Quinn asked of his new guest.

"You know better than to give it a name," Chef growled at him. He immediately disapproved of the affinity the young man had for the animals. They were food - not pets.

The turtle lurched forward on its pectoral fins towards Quinn who instinctively leapt backwards towards the wall. The wooden board gave way, spilling the young man unceremoniously into a hidden compartment. Startled, Quinn scrambled to his feet only to notice the particularly sour look on Chef's face. Turning, he gasped as he looked directly into the eyes of an equally surprised woman. Her hair cascaded down her shoulders and his gaze traveled to the revealing curve of her neckline toward the cleavage of her breasts exposed above her tunic.

Chef shook his head and muttered under his breath as he walked over to the otherwise oblivious man. "Come on, we need to talk." Chef grabbed an entranced Quinn by the arm and shoved him backwards while he began to replace the boards to the hidden compartment. The woman smiled shyly at Quinn, who was rapidly blushing under this thick beard.

"SHHHHHH, don't say a word, and I mean it!" Chef whispered ominously in his ear as they both walked down to the doctor's office after he finished repairing the hidden compartment. They entered without knocking and the physician was in his chair peering through his glasses as he cleaned some instruments. He glanced up in surprise at the unexpected intrusion.

"Doc, we have a bloody damn problem! Quinn has stumbled upon our little secret." Pixie leaned against the wall with his arms crossed. A heavy sigh escaped his lips. All had been going so well up to this point.

In contrast to the man's extreme irritation, the doctor leaned back in his chair and examined his glasses as he considered his words before speaking. "Quinn, you know that having a woman aboard ship is strictly forbidden. The Captain would be very angry if he found out and would punish us severely, including her. Her very life depends on you keeping our little secret."

"Why is she here?" He still could barely comprehend what he had just witnessed. The curve of her bosom was etched in his memory. Her gentle smile had completely mesmerized him.

"We are providing passage around the Horn. For a fee, of course," the doctor explained, wondering if his naïve friend had caught his drift.

"How did you get her aboard?" Quinn still was wide-eyed and questioning.

"She was smuggled inside of one of the food barrels. Do you remember the special shipment from the dock?" William glanced at Pixie who was still scowling from the sideline.

The three men looked at each other. "Have you ever been with a girl?" the doctor looked directly towards at Quinn.

Blood rushed to his cheeks, making them redder than normal. He averted his eyes and stammered. "Well --- uhhh, well, not really."

"Well Pixie, I believe we have an answer to our problem." William smiled sweetly. Yes, problem solved.

CHAPTER 13

Death on the Ocean

unting was once again prosperous after the ship rounded the tip of South America and pushed northward into the Pacific Ocean. The ship's bell rang as the whalers pulled into a South American port. Pixie was excruciatingly somber as the crew moored the vessel and irritated at Quinn's excitement to go ashore.

"Come on, Pixie. This should be exciting. An expedition with the doctor to get more coca leaves." Quinn was busy deciding what to take on the quest. Suddenly he quieted when he noticed a large barrel had been pushed into the middle of the galley. "Oh – is our guest leaving us?"

The cook locked the door to the galley and gave a large sigh. Calling to the woman in the hidden room, he brought her over to the barrel. Pixie had clearly become enamored with her and he kissed her long and deep enough for Quinn to turn and study the cutlery on the wall. Slowly he helped her into the barrel and secured the lid.

"Okay, let's go before I decide otherwise." Pixie hoisted the barrel onto a dolly and they excited to the chase boat.

The doctor was already in the small craft awaiting the rest of the crew. He looked ruggedly handsome with his satchel draped over his shoulder. A magnifying glass hung around his neck. He met Chef's eyes and also gazed at the barrel that was going ashore with some other supplies. Upon reaching the dock, the doctor and a small contingent of men including Quinn split company and headed up the valley and up the hillside into the deep forest.

"What exactly are we looking for?" Quinn's job was to help the doctor. The other men kept a lookout for any hostiles. Although this port was considered relatively friendly, one always had to keep alert when traveling away from town.

"Coca leaves. A small green leaf that is grey on the underside. They smell a bit like tea." The doctor expertly approached a bushy tree with small light yellow flowers. "Here we are, put these in the satchels."

"Pixie has been making tea with these leaves for the Captain every day. He does not look well and has not been finishing his meals." Quinn knew the health of the Captain of the boat weighed heavily on the doctor. "What is wrong with him?"

"I believe he has blood poisoning from when he injured his leg. I have tried everything I know. I even read that turtle saliva has medicinal properties from chewing the seaweed. That's why I have been swabbing their mouths from time to time." The doctor filled his bag and was relieved to have found the source of coca. He was running preciously low on his reserves and had postponed elective procedures for fear of running out.

Returning to town, they finished trading for fresh fruits and vegetables. Being a perishable item, the crew might go weeks and months without the food item and many men had permanent changes to both their teeth and bones from chronic deficiency. Quinn returned to the ship and spent the next several hours stowing the new supplies. Soon they were underway and back to the job of hunting whales.

Drowning his sorrow in a glass of rum, Chef called to his red-haired helper. "Hey, choose one of the turtles. I believe we need a special meal tonight."

Quinn dreaded this moment. He had been responsible for the animals' care and had developed an affinity for the creature's quiet nature. Both animals were munching their plant food while Quinn quickly averted his eyes and gathered the larger turtle, saving his favored Club for another time. They are food, he kept reminding himself, knowing that he could not partake in the evening's meal.

Pixie had avoided using the animals, knowing it would upset Quinn. But he was much more pragmatic than his sensitive friend and he had a secondary motive. He wanted to offer the Captain something different as the man had become thin and pale and his appetite waned. The doctor was worried about his health. Although the man's leg wound had finally healed on the surface, their leader continued to sicken. First mate Avery had taken over many of his duties while he rested.

Chef sent Quinn on an errand while he began to prepare the turtle for cooking. After taking the animal's life, he flipped the sea creature on its back and popped off the bottom plate to remove the internal organs. Quinn had returned when Chef called to him. "Hey, I think I know why Club's shell is curved underneath. This one had eggs in her and must be the female." What a bonus, he thought and was quite pleased as he proceeded to cook the turtle right in her shell.

Quinn tried to not let any feelings cloud his exterior features. They had to eat to survive and he knew that. But the vision of the mother whale and baby danced in the edges of his memories. "I hope the Captain likes the meal," he said thinly, trying to pay homage to the turtle's ultimate sacrifice.

That evening, the Captain did his best to enjoy the dinner. His laugh was hearty, but the spark in his eye was dimming. He was losing his strength and vitality. The aches seemed greater and he was so tired. He knew his destiny was to die upon the ocean where he loved to be. He regretted that he would never see his family again but felt there was no better place to meet his maker.

After several bedridden days, the Captain died in his sleep. William had watched over his old friend, spooning him special medicine made from his coca supply to ease his pain. When he took his last labored breath, the doctor felt a cool shiver over his shoulders. Half-expecting to see Quinn's angel, he glanced around the room. Seeing nothing, he returned his gaze to his old friend. "I sure hope she came for you," he said.

"How should I note his death in the ship's log?" Avery had lingered in the corner for the past several minutes.

"I believe it was metal poisoning," replied the doctor. "Probably from the injury he sustained during the wave. I tried to get every piece out. He must have absorbed some into his bloodstream." The doctor was torn as his long-time colleague and friend had slowly died before him.

"We should perform a burial as soon as possible. Are you able? Or do I need to perform the ceremony?"

"No, I am quite able." William returned to his office, not feeling up to the task at all.

The burial day was blustery as the entire crew stood at attention. William read a verse from the Bible and each man lowered his chin in reverence.

"Goodbye my old friend, travel well." The doctor held his hand to the Captain's head covered by the canvas for just a moment. They had been together a long time. Avery gave the nod, and the body slipped into the clutches of the sea. He then ordered the bark to turn the ship's direction to the South and head home. Such was the protocol when the Captain died.

The somber crew continued with their duties. Quinn sat across from Club before retiring for the evening. He had run out of plants to feed him although the animal seemed content. Gazing into his gentle eyes, the turtle seemed almost human. He found himself thinking of his father. One of his biggest regrets was that the man never knew what had happened to him. "I am so sorry father – I had no choice." A tear traversed his cheek. He found himself thinking of his brother. Was he still alive?

The turtle put his head into Quinn's hand and he cupped his

friend under its chin as reflected on his life. He began his whaling career as a prisoner. His soul bled for every whale that was slaughtered, but that had become his way of life. His destiny was set. But he did have the power to change the outcome of the creature in front of him. All energies, no matter how large or small, have the right to exist. There had to be more to life than simple survival. Seeing the dolly stacked with the evening's trash, he got up and brought the wooden cart over. Tipping Club onto his shell, he placed him against the supports and covered him with a cloth. The night was dark and most men were hovered around the fire drums.

Although his heart was beating madly, he took a deep breath and nonchalantly rolled the cart near the back of the ship, casually dumping the contents overboard into the dark inky water. "Travel well, my friend." Knowing there would be some hell to pay, he returned to his bed with a lighter heart.

Morning came quickly as work in the galley got underway. Pixie's eyebrows were arched and his eyes were sharp with reprimand when Quinn rounded the corner. He looked to the vacant pen in the corner.

"I let him go." Quinn had no choice but to tell the truth. He tried to explain his reasoning to the Chef. "I was thinking of the Captain, my Father, my life in general. I just felt it was the right thing to do."

"Damn you, now you have done it. I have to report this to Avery. I can only hope he is in a reasonable mood. Maybe I can say the wretched animal was sick or something. Yea, the Captain did pass after we ate the other one. Maybe that will be sufficient." Chef tried to sound mad, but he was actually quite worried. Quinn's actions could easily carn him a death penalty. Approaching Avery, he settled for an honest explanation.

Avery listened and groaned inwardly. Would his first act as Captain be to deliver a death sentence? They were already down men and he could not afford to lose an excellent bosun. He did not really care about the turtle. The crew had come to call the animal by a name from a deck of cards. However, he had to meter some sort of punishment. Relieved he had a line of reason for his decision, he settled on six hard lashes of the whip.

Pixie returned to the galley and delivered the good news. "Bless that man, he has been mighty generous. Six lashes from the whip. You might lose some skin, but at least you will not lose your life." He seemed genuinely relieved. "Besides, I am used to you being here. It would ruin my workload to lose you now."

Quinn dutifully presented himself for punishment. Removing his shirt, they started to tie him to the post but Quinn told them it wasn't necessary. The entire crew watched as his crime was called out and the leather whip brought to bear. Each lashing was strong and cut deeply into his exposed skin. Quinn accepted every penance and felt at peace with his actions.

Later in the privacy of the infirmary, the doctor tended his wounds. "What in hell has gotten into you?" He spoke gruffly but gently applied a salve. "You bled all over the floor."

"I'll clean it up, don't worry." As close as they were, he did not expect his friend to understand about releasing the animal. Quinn grimaced as he pulled his shirt over his raw back. Leaning down, he had déjà-vu thinking of the whale's blood on the deck. He scraped some of his own blood into a cloth before bringing over the mop and cleaning the floor. Bidding goodnight, he left for the galley and his room.

"Hey Quinn, come over here." Isaac, one of the oldest whalers on the boat, called to him. "I want you to have this." He placed a flat piece of bone into his hands, the size of a dinner plate. "This is from her, the mother whale. Do you know of which I speak?"

"Of course I do. She haunts my dreams at times." Quinn caressed the bone in his hand. The surface was oddly smooth. He smiled at the older man and emotion choked any further conversation.

"You deserve it." The sailor turned to leave but pivoted back around. "I am glad you released him," he whispered quietly and walked away.

After returning to his own bunk, Quinn looked for the small jar which contained the dried blood of the mother and baby whale from that fateful day eons ago. Carefully adding his congealed blood into the container, he mixed the contents together and placed it back onto the shelf. Taking the whale bone, he held it tight against his chest. With some remnant of closure, he rolled onto his stomach and attempted to sleep though the night.

CHAPTER 14

The New Captain

The whaler finally returned to the New Bedford harbor. Swinging high in his bosun's chair, Quinn gazed out across the bay. The ships were to his left and the bodies of the whales to the right. Smoke coming from the chimneys could be seen on the hill past the wharf. He pulled his jacket closer around his neck as the chilly wind lifted his collar and caressed his back. It had taken months for the boat to return to port and they arrived in the middle of winter. Even his breath turned into frozen vapor in the breeze.

He had held the whale bone several times over the past few weeks, needle in hand yet he remained undecided on where to make the first etching. Studying the ship moored before him, he noted every mast and line. He had always fancied being a writer and storyteller. Having no pen and paper, perhaps he could tell his story in his pictures.   The birds squawked noisily around his position and he was reminded of the hummingbird visit and the way it cocked its head when it looked at him. Yes, he had the first inspiration for his carving on the scrimshaw.

"Hey, the boat is returning." Quinn's attention turned to the man who was astride a cross beam like he was riding a horse. Quinn and the other crew came down to the deck as the small boat came closer to the hull.

"Is that our new Captain?" Murmurs came from the gathering crew.

"I'm not sure, but it looks like it." Everybody was aware they had returned to port to be assigned a new leader. Avery was quite proficient but would remain as first mate.

The man out of the boat quickly scaled the ladder, refusing any attempts to be assisted aboard. His cold blue eyes were sharp with attention. His scraggly beard barely covered his pitted skin. His age was deceptive. Although his hair was grey, one couldn't tell if he was older.

He silently appraised his new crew. With no emotion portrayed, he addressed the group standing at attention. "I am Master of this vessel." He walked casually along the line of men, looking at each sailor and not breaking eye contact until some sign of deference was shown. Two thick-set men followed behind him, and Avery unhappily brought up the rear. "My bosun will inform you of my rules and regulations. Together we will make this boat profitable. Obey me, and we will get along. Disobey me, and punishment will be swift and severe. Avery, show me my quarters," he commanded of his first officer. "Then get this ship cleaned up in tip-top shape!"

"This way, sir." The officer nodded quickly as he motioned the group.

Quinn breathed a sigh of relief as the group fell from sight. "I have never seen Avery look so unhappy. What do you know about our new Captain?"

The chef knit his eyebrows together. "I heard he is a hard man." Actually, rumors from the bar in town were not encouraging but he did not want to alarm his crew mates. He certainly did not like the looks of the two recruits who flanked the man. "It's freezing out here. Help me get the meal started. I better impress our new commander."

Quinn was finishing putting away the cutlery when Chef steamed into the kitchen. "Damn buggar!" he cursed under his breath. His face was flushed and his eyes sparked with anger.

"What happened, how was dinner?"

"Oh, just fine. Appears the Captain likes the food well enough but he had me linger in the corner like the wait staff. I went to sit down and he said only officers sit at the table. Oh, and by the way, you have been fully demoted from bosun. His men will be in charge of the deck now. They are here to protect the Captain as well."

"What, they are enforcers?" Quinn was getting a knot in his stomach.

"He had the gall to say our old Captain was too soft on us. That the company demanded he whip us into shape. He will be conducting drills in the morning. He is a cold man. I don't like him, and I don't even know him yet." Pixie was clearly irritated as he continued to murmur under his breath.

Quinn retired to his bunk. Taking out the precious jawbone, he moved the light closer to study the surface. Just having the piece in his hand calmed him. Chef's ranting had put him on edge. Taking a finely chiseled sliver of bone, he started to etch the ship in the bay from memory. The hard surface resisted the first strokes, but then seemed to acquiesce to the will of the artist. The tip quickly dulled as each line was placed. Sharpening was required after only three furrows. This was slow and tedious work, but it relaxed his mind. Struggling to see his progress, Quinn had a moment of inspiration. Retrieving the dried blood concoction from the shelf and mixing in ash, he rubbed the material into crevices created by his needle and the picture began to reveal itself.

Pleased with his progress, he started to blow out his oil lamp. On second thought, he reached into his pocket for a collection of small bones. He had carved them long ago, slowly acquiring each piece. The boys had used them for their dice games. He also had developed the knack of throwing them into the air and reading a fortune based on how they landed. When many of his predictions came to pass, the crew around him became slightly suspicious. When he burned his cheek with the charge, some of the crew said he was marked. That was the turning point to grow as thick a beard as possible. Now Quinn consulted his carvings only in private. Gently rubbing them in his hand to create heat, he concentrated on his question. How would the boat fare under their new Captain? Opening his hand, he gently tossed them to the desk, watching them jockey for position. Even as they settled, one stone rolled back to its side as if undecided. Either way, the story did not look promising. In fact, the reading was outright bleak if he interpreted them correctly. What a stupid game, he chided himself as he returned the bones to his pocket.

CHAPTER 15

The Grapes

A commotion above deck garnered the interest of those in the galley. The men stopped their work as the cries of a crewmate did not cease.

"Go see what's going on." Pixie had become much less jovial.

Quinn stuck his head out the galley door in time to see the bosun hauling some of the newest recruits by the scruff, one in each hand. Shock and fear gripped the faces of two boys. The company continued to fill whaling spots on the boat in the same manner that Quinn had been forced to join. The man gruffly tore a small bag from the youngest one's hand and exposed its contents. "Grapes, where in the hell did you get grapes?!"

The boy stammered, tears rushing down his face. "I had them with me when they took me. They were in my pocket. I did not steal them, they were mine. The other boy tried to take them from me."

The man held both boys so tightly they dropped to their knees in pain. All mumbling ceased as the Captain strolled out onto the deck. "What appears to be the problem here?"

The situation was explained as the boys peered up at the Captain.

"You are both thieves. In fact, you did steal from me, as everything on this boat is mine, including those grapes you brought aboard. Do you hear that?" The Captain rotated around and spoke to the entire crew. "Everything aboard belongs to me, even your petty lives." He returned his intense gaze onto the boys in front of him. "Remove their clothing and tie them to the posts."

The boys were unceremoniously stripped and secured to a

mast. For once, Quinn was grateful he had been removed of his bosun title. The man who took his place gladly pulled out the whip he kept secured to his belt. With a nod, the Captain strode back to his room as the beating began.

The first lash caused both boys to scream out in pain. Each successive whipping evoked more sobbing but eventually the crying stopped all together and the boys hung limply from their ropes. The entire crew watched in shocked silence as the man wiped human flesh from his whip and holstered it to his side. "Everybody get back to work," he commanded of those around him.

"Cut them down and bring them to my office." The doctor's voice challenged from the back of the gathered crowd. Men parted and the stately tall man stared eye-to-eye with the bosun. Thick tension hung in the air as the two men silently sized each other up. The crew breathed an inward sigh of relief when the bosun broke eye contact, spun on his heel and strode away. The doctor looked for Quinn and motioned him to release the lifeless bodies from their tethers.

Quinn and another man carried the unconscious boys into the infirmary, placing them face down on the table.

"God what a mess this is." William was disgusted. "There is such a thing as punishment by whipping, but this is criminal." His hands shook with the fury contained within. "What am I supposed to do with this? There is no skin left on this boy's back."

He looked down at the smaller boy. He was really just a child. Freckles and light brown hair and he did not even know his name. The bosun had whipped almost every inch of his backside. Could one even recover from such injuries?

With Quinn's assistance, the doctor wrapped the wounds in salve and bandages and had them placed in one of the lower holds. Getting two small tumblers, he poured a small drink for them both.

"Do you think they will survive?" Quinn was stunned at the severity of their punishment.

"They probably will wish they could die once they regain consciousness, if they do." William studied the glass as he slowly rotated his drink on the table. "You know the two men that Captain put in the hold the other week for seven days? Turns out, he ordered no food or water. They were barely alive when that gorilla of a bosun brought them here. I could not do anything for them. They paid for very minor offenses with their lives. I understand that discipline is necessary and the death penalty has been administered for severe cases, but this is getting ridiculous."

The doctor put away the tumblers as somebody knocked at the door and the chef stepped into the room. He sat down heavily into a chair and eyed the bottle. Bringing out a small glass, the doctor offered him some drink.

"What's bothering you, Pixie?" the doctor asked.

"That is what's bothering me." He pointed at the leftover bandaging on the floor. "I heard those two men who died last week were placed in the brig for not polishing their shoes correctly. That is absolute abuse!"

"Hold your voice down." The doctor motioned Quinn to check the door and make sure it was sealed. "I know it has been bad since he came on board but we have to be careful. Maybe he will settle down. Just don't do anything to get in trouble and let us pray it gets better soon."

The men split company and the doctor mused over his drink. Then he crushed some coca leaves to take down to the injured boys. They would be in dear need of some pain relief if they lived.

Nantucket Boat Ride

Quinn had just delivered the doctor his lunch and sat down briefly in the chair. The Captain would have found it disdainful if he knew the two shared meals together at times. The bosun seemed to watch everybody and Quinn found his visits somewhat curtailed.

"No whales sighted so far. I imagine that is a relief for you although not good for the profession in general." The doctor studied the young man. He had been stressed for days, ever since being called before the bosun.

Whales had been scarce lately. Although sperm whales were the quarry of desire, all of the great cetaceans were fair game now. With hundreds of whaling vessels on the ocean, the unthinkable had happened. The population was dwindling.

The bosun had recently called a meeting of all the laymen. He had addressed Quinn directly. "I notice you do not go out on the chase crafts. That is going to change with the next hunting excursion. You are in the larboard aft group." The boats were named for their position on the gangway. He retrieved several straws from his pocket and handed them to the remaining group of men. "Anyone with a short straw needs to stand over here."

A group of men separated themselves and the bosun assigned positions. Head harpooner Charles looked displeased. In the past, he had his own crew, trained the way he wanted them. This new procedure of constant shuffling of personnel made him tense. Men did not know the procedure and opportunities were lost due to incompetence at times. The current captain looked poorly on failure. He had voiced his concern once, only to be met with silence and arched eyebrows.

Back in the infirmary, Quinn stood up to leave when the ship's bell rang, signaling everyone to their stations. Dread filled his heart as he looked to the doctor.

"You will be okay. It's just this one time." William tried to buoy his friends' spirits.

Quinn arrived on deck and made his way to the stern. Three boats were being made ready for the chase. He glanced at the harpooner. A large muscular man with a stone face sized him up. A necklace of bones and teeth was tethered around his neck. "You will be the caller." The two of them had hardly exchanged words during his time as a whaler but he knew this particular man was known for his feral instincts during the hunt.

Each sailor was assigned to their station and slid down the rope after the mate and harpooner stepped into the craft. Quinn sat down directly under the officer manning the tiller. The day was windy and spray was already making him wet. The insecurity of the small craft caused him to grab the edges of the seat. Taking a deep breath and sensing the cadence of the boat, he began to chant at the men, creating a synchronous unit between the oars.

The men strained against their extra long paddle, one per seat from the far side of the boat. If the whales were at a distance, a sail could be unfurled to help save energy. Coming in under wind also aided in not spooking the whales. However, these animals were already on the run and close enough that the mate in charge chose to pursue under manpower.

Quinn watched as the boats gained access to their prey. Although he abhorred hunting in general, he could not help but get caught up in the excitement. He recognized the whales as a smaller variety called Minkes. Although largely ignored in the beginning of the industry, it was discovered their oil had a different viscosity which was thicker and burned longer.

The boat ran directly behind the pod and the harpooner stood and braced himself. Taking one of two irons up over his shoulder as the boat bumped against the creature, he flexed and plunged the odd-shaped harpoon point deeply into the side.

"AWAY," the mate called from the tiller as the whale thrashed from the injury and each man frantically reversed his oar as the enraged creature responded to the insult by swinging its great tail and then dove deep into the ocean. The specially coiled rope whirred as it disappeared over the lip and all the men crowded to the back of the boat to add ballast as the whale dragged them through the heavy swell. Soon the bow was pulled treacherously towards the surface and the mate called for the extra rope. A sailor grabbed the line from another bucket and handed it to the harpooner who secured the new length and released the original tether from its latch.

"Ahhhh − oh God, I'm stuck," a sailor screamed as he was dragged towards to the front of the boat. The harpooner tackled the man as he was catapulted forward and held his arm as the rope squeezed up his hand and tightened around his finger. Flesh burned as the rope continued over the side.

"Quickly, secure the line off in front of me," the harpooner sneered to the crew. He could not afford to lose this whale, not under this captain. A sailor grabbed a bar and after making a twist, levered the instrument in the bow to release tension on the rope so the man could be released.

Quinn went forward to help the man, only to be restrained from the mate in charge. "Stay in your position, there is nothing you can do for him."

The bow once again dipped into the wave but the whale surfaced nearby, mortally wounded and tired from its valiant effort. The mate stepped forward and the man with the necklace took control of the tiller. Taking a large lance, the officer aimed for lung tissue and plunged the point deep into the beast. Although red already stained the whale's breath, a new surge of blood expelled on the next blow and soon the creature rolled and died.

Quinn sat frozen in his seat. Sorrowful whale sounds seemed to resonate in the waters below the hull of the small boat. Every hair on his body was erect as a shiver passed through his body. The injured man cradled his hand and appeared to be in shock. The mate returned to his station at the stern while rope was pulled back in.

Startling him out of his thoughts, the officer commanded Quinn. "Help him to the back, then take his place on the oar."

Quinn did as directed and grabbed a saltwater soaked cloth and gently wrapped the man's hand as he assisted him to the stern. Then returning to the vacated seat, he took the oar in his hands and proceeded to help tow the deceased whale back to the ship. A flurry of birds erupted from the empty spaces of the sky and fins were visible in the water, no doubt attracted by the blood. The other boats soon joined them with a catch in tow, a successful hunt indeed.

Upon securing the whale to the cutting deck, the crew was finally allowed to disembark. Quinn assisted the injured man up the ropes and the officer in charge did not question his actions. William was waiting in the infirmary, already notified there had been injuries.

"What do we have?" The doctor queried Quinn as they entered.

"His hand was caught in the rope. The bone is exposed on his finger."

The doctor un-wrapped the cloth as Quinn retrieved the box of curved blades and handed them to the physician. Then he gave the injured man a small amount of rum and some coca leaves to chew.

"There is no saving this. But you are lucky. It's only a finger, and not the entire hand." William studied the bruised and bloodied appendage and felt grateful. A man could do without a finger, but losing an entire hand was quite a disability. Choosing a curved blade from the box, he expertly felt for the rounding of the bone at the joint. Quinn applied the tourniquet and the doctor made the incision between the bones, cutting backwards and leaving some skin. Then he identified the vessels and pinched them between the tips of an instrument. Using a flame against the metal, he sealed the bleeders. Carefully sewing the flaps of skin over the severed finger, the doctor motioned Quinn to apply the bandage.

Later with just the two of them, William brought out the glasses and the rum. "So, how was it?"

"It was gruesome. Between the man being caught in the rope and the whale thrashing around, it was beyond description. The harpooner and the mate were not going to lose that whale. I think they would have sacrificed poor ole Bob before losing that rope. Everybody is so afraid of our Captain. They know he will punish them for missing."

"I was hoping the man would lighten up in his tactics. Appears he is quite the disciplinarian. Just stay out of trouble, my friend." William ushered Quinn from his office and cleaned the floors himself.

CHAPTER 17

The Transcending Light

The Captain passed a new rule. No one was allowed to have a personal lamp. Lamps required whale oil, therefore lighting one was considered stealing from the company. Quinn had to suspend work on his whalebone. The carving of the ship had sprung to life and in his next story he was busy telling was that of Charles and his rowers chasing after the whale. His friend stood tall in the front of the small boat with his spear ready. However, he did not dare light a lantern for his work.

The men would cluster around the barrels in the evening, the only source of heat and light allowed. On one particularly dark night, the bosun shouted as he hauled a man above deck. Quinn's heart sank as he saw one of the few boys from his original days in the holds be placed in front of the captain. The bosun held an oil lamp in his hand. "I caught this man with a lamp below deck."

"I was retrieving stores from below," the panicked man stuttered as he attempted to defend himself. "I had to see what I was doing. I was following orders to have this job completed today."

"Perhaps you should have made the repairs when it was light out." The bosun snarled back at the shaken man.

"I am sorry but I did not have time with all the jobs I had to do."

The Captain sauntered from his cabin to assess the situation. He smiled as he looked around at the nervous crew. "I have a question. Can an oil lamp stay lit under water?" When no one answered, he offered "I know, let us perform an experiment. Bring rope and a casement from the armory." He pointed to a man who dashed to fulfill the request.

Perplexed where this was heading, the crew watched as the unfortunate man was led to the side of the boat. The bosun held the accused man tightly while his colleague reached down and secured his feet to the casement. Then taking the left over rope, they tied his hands around the handles of the still burning lamp.

"So, how long will the lamp burn?" the Captain again addressed the crew. "Well, let's see." With a kick of his foot, he shoved the bound casement into the water. As the rope uncoiled and tightened around the surprised man's legs, the bosun dropped him over the side. The flame of the lamp extinguished immediately with the splash and the sailor disappeared into the sea. A gasp escaped the astonished men, but not a word was uttered.

"Hmmm, apparently not long." The Captain stated loudly while looking into the water. "You will not disobey me. I hope this teaches you all a lesson that you will never forget."

Quinn felt his pulse pound in his head. Rage filled him and his fingernails dug holes into his palms. Looking around, he met the eyes of his fellow sailors. Many of them had been together for years, suffered hardships, and even though they may have had some strife with one another, they were family. On the ship, the Captain has full autonomy to do whatever he pleases. Their previous Captain had been fair, and they had loved him for it. This man was pure evil. The crowd dispersed silently to their stations.

"Quinn," Chef approached him back in the galley. "I am sorry. I know he was your friend."

Quinn could not reply. Overpowering sorrow was laced with feelings of anger. He could not remember being more angry in all his life.

"Hey, throw your bones for me. What's our fate under this captain?" Chef occasionally asked to have his fortune told.

Quinn gathered the small artifacts from his pocket and let them fall to the top of a box. Shaking his head solemnly, he replied, "death," and walked silently away.

CHAPTER 18

Retribution

he crew was sullen and unhappy. Instead of instilling work ethic and obedience, resentment burned in the hearts of the men. One day out at sea, two whaling vessels came side to side. Bartering was common practice between boats.

The Captain was on deck, studying a large net of fish for purchase. He personally checked every load, examining the fish for freshness and quality. "What do we have here?"

"Aye Captain, you have a sharp eye. That's a stingray. Rare to catch one in the fish net you know. They make excellent eating." The quartermaster of the sister ship brought over a wooden box of produce. "I have something really special as well, fresh fruit. Just the thing to keep the scurvy away."

The Captain looked greedily at the beautiful robust grapes and motioned for the net to be unloaded. He directed the box towards his galley master. "This is for me."

Chef personally took over storing the provisions. "Be bloody well careful of the ray. Let me handle it." Taking a grappling hook, he held down the writhing animal from a distance to avoid its tail whipping back and forth and delivered the death blow. "Tonight we are having ray soup."

Harvesting the wings into pieces, he set them into a pan of fat, salt and seasonings. Soon a bubbling concoction filled the air with a promise of fresh food for officers and crew alike. Chef carefully wrapped the severed tail with heavy material and handed it to Quinn. "Take this to the Doc. Be careful and don't fall down." He smugly laughed, remembering the man's unfortunate incident with the harpoon. His face became more serious. "I mean it though."

"What does he want with this?" Quinn turned the item back and forth in his hand.

"He said something about ancient Greek medicine and numbing for teeth and gums. He was particularly adamant that I save it for him without damaging it. Here, take these also." Pixie looked around carefully and then took a small bunch of grapes from the Captain's box. "He asked me for a few grapes with his night cap. Keep them hidden for God's sakes. Our leader would gladly have our hides if he caught you with them in your pocket."

Quinn gently tapped on the doctor's door as he entered. William peered up from his glasses. "Ahh - thank you, my boy." He smiled when he noticed the cloth package which contained the tail. "Put that in the cabinet with my other trinkets of interest," he instructed. "If it starts to smell I will just toss it out my window." He laughed heartily and they chatted for a moment and whispered. "Come have a drink. Was the Chef able to get me a bit of fruit?"

Taking out the cups, Doc poured just a dash of the rum as Quinn retrieved the grapes from his pocket and put them on the desk. Taking one, the older man rolled it in his hand before handing it to his friend. "Bottoms up," he proclaimed and each of them savored the sweet flesh and succulent juice.

"Now it's time for me to retire." Doc took off his glasses and rubbed his temples. "I'll see you tomorrow."

As soon as Quinn left the room, the doctor quietly locked the door. Putting back on his glasses, he retrieved the stingray's poisonous tail from the shelf and un-wrapped it on the table. After careful examination, he removed the ominous spine that was attached midway. Being a doctor of many years, he had ample opportunity to see the excruciating effects the toxin contained within. Using a small chisel, he scraped the grooves on either side of the serrated appendage and mixed the contents into a previously prepared bowl of whale oil.

The Captain had not relented in his governing style over the

past several months. In all his years on the ocean, he had never experienced unfairness to this degree. He seethed over the death of
the small boy who had been whipped. The larger boy recovered and
would have the pain of his scars the rest of his life. The younger had
struggled valiantly and pleaded for help. Infection finally proved the
victor and his body was released to the sea.

During a port excursion for supplies, the doctor met secretly with
acquaintances from another ship. The company would do nothing
to replace this new commander. The boat was surprisingly profitable
under his command. They only cared about the bottom line. The
men had quietly talked and money exchanged hands. An idea in the
doctor's mind became a plan.

He gently pulverized the harvested spine material and warmed
the mixture under a flame. He had been warned as too much heat
would inactivate the poison. God, would this even work? Taking a
fine piece of cloth, he strained the fluid into a bowl to remove any
particulate. Placing the six remaining grapes in front of him, he used
a bloodletting needle to inject the permeated whale oil into the body
of each grape. He shook his head at the irony of having this particular fruit for his vehicle. Had he told his illicit friend the story? Or was
it just coincidence? Either way, what a fitting end for the Captain.
He hoped it worked. If not, he might very well be the next body over
the railing.

The next day, the doctor went to the galley right before lunch.
One thing about Chef was his timing about meals.

"What can I do for you, Doc? Quinn was going to bring your
meal in about an hour."

"I am in need of a cup of coffee. I did not sleep well last night."
William leaned against the wall, sipping the hot beverage and chat-
ting idly as he watched the cook prepare the officer's plates.

Taking a handful of grapes from the wooden box, Pixie arranged
them on the Captain's plate. The Captain was the only officer to re-
ceive the fruit. The doctor turned to leave and casually walked by

the dish, discretely adding the six contraband grapes from his pocket to the mix. Leaving the room, he could feel his pulse pounding. He prayed no one would be snitching the fruit on the way to the man's table. Panic gripped him momentarily as he considered the possibility of sickening someone by accident but Chef personally delivered the meal intact. The Captain always ate alone in his cabin and only an empty plate was returned to the kitchen.

William spent the afternoon attempting to stay busy. Quinn had brought him lunch and they chatted as usual. He had to maintain a normal appearance but he was nervous. He had helped men die before, but only to hasten imminent death and prevent further suffering. He had never experienced such shadow as the Captain possessed. If his plan went awry, the Chef and his staff would be incriminated. Would the man eat enough of the grapes? Would the toxin even work in this manner? How long would it take? Anxiety gnawed at his belly and it seemed an eternity for the dinner hour to arrive. Although the Captain ate his meals in his cabin, he still joined the officer table in the evening.

"Chef, get me some more rum." The Captain shifted in his chair. William studied him closely. Small beads of perspiration glistened on his forehead. Taking the offered glass, he emptied the alcohol in a few sips. "What is our total in the hold?" he questioned the quartermaster although he was not actually listening to the answer. Twirling his empty glass on the table, he continued to feign interest but finally just stood up. "Gentlemen, I believe I will turn in for the evening." All the men rose from their seats as he left the table.

In the middle of the night, a shipman pounded on Doc's door. "Hurry, the Captain is sick. Something is dreadfully wrong."

Grabbing his medical bag, William quickly ran to the Captain's bedside.

"What is wrong?" the bosun whispered in his ear.

"I don't know." The doctor began to examine the prone man.

He was covered in sweat and breathing in short staccato bursts. Foamy saliva ran down his chin. For a brief of moment, the dying man's eyes locked with the doctor and they stared at each other. A slight smile of acknowledgment and concession crossed the Captain's face as he passed. Did he know? Does an evil man instinctively recognize an evil deed?

Avery burst into the room. "What has happened?"

"The Captain has died. His heart appears to have had a seizure." William started to place the man's hands across his chest.

"Oh my God!" Avery went to the Captain's side. Even in death, his face looked ruthless. Avery had pleaded for many a man's life and unbeknownst to the crew, actually thwarted quite a few executions. Although he had no aspirations of being Captain, he wished desperately that he did not serve under this particular man.

"Doctor, are we close enough to port to return him for burial?" The first mate did not relish the idea of having his body on the ship any longer than necessary.

"No, we are too far away. A burial at sea is the only choice." The final part of William's plan was to make sure all evidence of the crime was disposed of properly.

"We will perform the ceremony tomorrow then." The officer left the stateroom, once again acting as Captain.

The next morning, Avery called the crew together and informed them of the new circumstance. The Captain's heart had failed and he would be acting Captain. They would head for home port.

The doctor presided over the burial, making an excellent show of reading from his holy book. Only dry eyes prevailed. As the body slipped into the sea, Quinn almost felt like clapping. Never had he despised a man so much. Morale had become so poor that shore excursions were not allowed for fear of mass desertions. Most Captains feared backlash from the men, but he suspected this Master would have relished a mutiny with glee. As the body splashed into the water, he wanted to yell out, "Yes." However, he maintained a somber exterior.

The Chef did not mind a breach in etiquette. He leaned to Quinn's ear and whispered, "Maybe there is a God after all."

CHAPTER 19

The Sabatier

The vessel arrived in port and the crew began maintenance duties while the whaling company decided on a new Captain. Quinn took out his prized scrimshaw for the first time in months. He had several days to work at his carving and was busy drawing a pod of whales in the distance. Nothing was more exhilarating than being high in the mast where he could study the great leviathans in their natural habitat. At that moment he was actually in charge of the direction of the ship. He held up his creation for a better look in the light. Not just a picture, but a letter that represented a chronicle of his life. He liked the fact that his own blood, along with the blood of the whales, was the life force of the piece. A piercing whistle grabbed his attention and he put his artwork away and headed to the deck to join the gathering crew.

They stood at attention as the small boat arrived with the officers and their new Captain. The man ascended the ladder and gratefully accepted the outstretched arm of the receiving deckhand. "Thank you," he said as he came aboard. His attire was immaculate and his light colored beard crisply trimmed. He keenly observed the crew, but his eyes held just a hint of kindness.

The doctor smiled and extended his hand. "Welcome aboard, sir." William looked at Avery, who looked quite pleased. This Master was rumored to have a good reputation for being able and fair.

Walking down the line, each crew member introduced themselves. As he came to Quinn, the Captain stopped. "I understand you were previously the bosun. Would you care for the job again?"

"Yes sir, it would be my honor." Quinn smiled in acceptance.

Quinn and Chef returned to the galley as the men dispersed

to their positions. "I have a good feeling about the new Captain." Chef started to rummage through his supplies, deciding on his meal plan. "I am so glad that last man is gone. The crew was about to self-destruct. I was worried we might have an uprising. Lucky for us he died so suddenly. I did not realize he was sick."

Yes, Quinn thought. The circumstances were interesting. Doc seemed nonchalant about the entire incident. Quinn asked him about the Captain's death but he had replied, "A man's heart can give out at any time." He did not put the wanderings of his thoughts to words and instead commented, "Avery looks very pleased as well. I have not seen him smile for months. "

"We are not putting out for a few weeks," said the chef. "I need some supplies in town if you can go tomorrow." Chef smiled to his helper and seemed quite chipper as he bounced about.

"Are you expecting a 'special shipment' again?" If there was going to be another woman in a barrel, Quinn wanted in from the beginning.

"Hmmm, wouldn't that be nice." Pixie grinned salaciously but then sighed heavily. "Nah, I have some shore leave in a few days. Hmm, maybe I can arrange something."

The next morning, Quinn set out for port. After spending the morning gathering items, he found himself looking once more into the window of the bookstore. How many years ago did he stand there, waiting for his brother. He was glad the business had managed to survive, as did the bar across the street. Studying his reflection in the window, he noted the heavily bearded face, wrinkles, and sun-drenched skin. Yes, a true whaler stared back at him. He heard footsteps behind him and this time immediately noted a man starting across the street. The man was dressed in an overcoat and hat and had just exited the bar. Quinn watched as the large oak door started to swing shut next to a large decorative anchor. The hinges of the heavy sign squeaked with the motion and Quinn studied the image of the two oil balers crossed over each other. The dark seedy interior was visible for only a moment.

The man angled towards Quinn. A hat covered most of his bearded face, but Quinn could see he was a man of stature. A mild accent revealed he was not from these parts.

"Are you attached to one of the ships?" His nose wrinkled as he acknowledged the smell of salt and whale oil coming from the man in front of him. Yes, Quinn was no doubt a whaler.

"Aye," Quinn vaguely pointed to the secondary pier where many boats were moored. "Who is asking?"

The stranger seemed disappointed. "Do you know anybody from that ship?" The man pointed to the left, towards a ship in place at the primary pier. As he raised his arm his jacket raised for a fraction of a second. Quinn could see a barrel under his jacket, approximately 18 inches tall with a small cylinder attached to the side.

Quinn looked at the boat, a mermaid adorned the bow. "No, I don't."

The man seemed to consider his options. "Do you want to make some extra money? I have a job if you are interested."

"What is the job?" Quinn studied his face. The man had a devious quality about him.

"You must first agree to the work. I cannot tell you otherwise." The gentleman seemed to have decided that Quinn was not his man and was already making to leave.

"No, thank you. I have to get back to my own crew."

They parted company and Quinn continued to the dock and began loading the supplies into a boat. Stopping to rest, he noticed the well-dressed man exiting the whaling vessel he had motioned to earlier. He walked confidently, exuding an air of "I belong here." His arms swung freely at his side and the barrel was no longer in his possession. What an odd man. Quinn knew better than to accept his offer earlier in the day but his interest was piqued.

"Any problems getting our supplies?" The Chef was glancing through the manifest back in the galley.

"None, but something strange happened on my way back." Quinn told Chef the story of the encounter with the stranger in town.

"Was the barrel large enough for a woman? Maybe you should have accepted the job." Chef laughed, quite pleased with his response.

Quinn shook his head in feigned disgust. "No, it was much smaller. There was a glass tube on the side. It was very strange." He looked downwards as he searched his memories. "I have never seen anything like it."

"Let it go and have something to eat. I may need help later to prepare dinner. I like the new Captain."

Quinn retired to his small room and pulled out the carving. The mother ship was complete and he was pleased with the intricate interplay of the riggings. Below the ship, Charles and his crew chased whales with spears lodged in their backs. He traced the etching with his finger, then took the quill and purposely poked his hand. Allowing a small drop of blood to stain the picture, he colored the spouting breath of the captured whale bright red. He stroked the pod of whales further up the scrimshaw, swimming fast to escape capture. Run, baby run, he crooned to them. At times, he could hear the whales through the wall of the ship. Placing a hollow tube to his ear helped amplify the sounds. He wondered what they were saying but suspected their song was steeped in sadness.

Suddenly, a loud boom radiated both through the water and the air. Startled, Quinn jumped from his seat as the floor trembled underneath him. Blowing out the lantern, he scrambled to the deck. "What happened?"

"There is a fire on the edge of town. The wharf is in flames and one of the ships has exploded. Over there in the first pier." One of his shipmates was already at the edge of the rail.

"Oh my God." Quinn was shocked to see that the boat with the mermaid was partially underwater. A huge fireball engulfed the entire ship which was quickly sinking. Barrels of oil were on fire near the pier and sirens were radiating through the town. Smoke soon choked the entire skyline and the crew maintained at ready in case they needed to cast from their mooring. He glanced around for Chef, his face ashen.

"You have to tell the Captain what you saw." Pixie had come up behind him and grabbed his arm, leading him to where the officers had gathered.

"Captain, I saw something in town today that may be important. A man propositioned me for a job. I declined but I could see he was hiding a small barrel under his jacket. I later saw him exiting the ship that just burned."

The Captain listened as Quinn recanted his interaction in town earlier in the day. He watched the burning ship and suspected the fire was far from accidental. The fire seemed to have started in a building on the edge of the wharf, but the ship had exploded. Politics had grown complex in the ports, and several players were always requesting payment to "stay safe." He had made it a habit through his career to try and make sure everybody was covered. As the bow slipped below the water line, he requested extra sentries be posted for the night.

After the evening's meal, Pixie and Quinn settled back in the galley with a small tumbler of rum. "I believe I see some smooth sailing ahead." The chef was basking in the glow of the Captain's pleasure of his cooking.

Quinn smiled and went to his bunk and privately pulled out his fortune bones. Feeling light of heart, he tossed them to the air. They settled in a disconcerting pattern. He frowned and shuffled them more completely and tried again. The pieces landed and Quinn was not pleased. Using his foot to swoosh them aside, he growled stupid game and extinguished his lamp.

The Scrimshaw

Quinn felt a renewed sense of purpose as the ship was outfitted for her next voyage. Being assigned bosun was a position of honor. As new whalers came aboard to replace those who disembarked for the last time, they greeted him with respect. He soon had men positioned all over the boat, mending, fixing, hammering or cleaning.

A crew member approached from the mast, his hands cupped together and held out in front of him. "I found this in one of the sails." He opened his fingers and exposed a baby bird. "There's an empty nest in one the riggings. What do I do with it?"

Quinn took the small creature into his palm. Grey skin covered its body and a scrawny neck could barely support the head. Tiny tubes which held the promise of feathers adorned its' side and back. The bird looked at him, then gaped open his beak for just a moment.

"I'll take care of him." Quinn glanced at the new man and nodded his appreciation. He had been surrounded by death for so long. It was incredibly refreshing for somebody to have a reverence for a life. Both men smiled as the bird repositioned in his hand, once again raising its open mouth upwards.

"I believe it's hungry. I guess a visit to the doctor is in order." Quinn grinned and turned to pay his friend William a visit.

"Enter," a voice commanded when Quinn knocked on the door. "What do you have there?"

"One of the men found a baby bird. It is very young and weak." Quinn set the creature down on the desk in front of the doctor.

William sat and studied the animal under arched eyebrows before meeting Quinn's eyes. The man in front of him had grown from adolescence into an admirable human being. Although he felt the best thing would be to put the poor creature out of its misery, he knew that would not be an option.

"Well, surprisingly, I do know what to do." He took part of his meal and added some water, making a moist sticky ball. Then using a small spatula, he stroked the side of the beak. "Come on baby, open up." When the bird finally did as commanded, he placed the food deep into its throat on the right side. "Just small amounts at first and you have to get it past the airway. Soon our friend will figure out what we are doing."

The Doctor stood to find a small flat pail, and lined it with cloth. "Put him, or her, in this and place it next to the lamp to keep him warm," he instructed Quinn.

"Okay, George, get comfy in your new home." Quinn grinned up at William. "That was the name of my dog growing up."

"Don't get too excited yet. I still have to discuss with the Captain if it's okay." The doctor would ask over dinner. Pets were discouraged on boats, but occasionally permission was giving as long as they did not affect the food supply. He smiled at the irony. Birds actually ate a tremendous amount in comparison to their small body size.

The next few weeks were a flurry of activity as the ship prepared to leave. Quinn spent his lunch time in the infirmary with William and little George. He marveled at how the bird was finally able to get his long legs under him. The tubular casings gave way to black feathers that unfurled daily.

"The crew has been calling you the 'bird doctor' since George has taken to riding on your shoulder." Quinn watched the crow as he bobbed up and down, excited at the younger man's arrival but not willing to leave his perch near the doctor's ear.

"I hate to admit it, but I am rather fond of him. I know he will probably fly away one day when his desires kick in. I hear we are headed further north this time. Whaling may soon become a way of the past. Some of the companies have sold their shares since petroleum was discovered and the unthinkable has happened. The population of whales is dwindling." The doctor filled the two tumblers and held a toast. "To the end of whaling."

"Yes," Quinn echoed. "To the end of whaling."

Quinn returned to his bunk and held his carving to the light. The bone was worn smooth on the edges from being worked in his hands. Tracing the large ship in the foreground, he could feel the cool air as he stood in the mast that day. Thinking of Charles standing proud in his chase boat, he thought of his unlikely friendship with the man. A smile crossed his face as he touched the small fluke exposed from the water he had chiseled in tribute next to the second smaller vessel. He bore the discomfort of his scars on his back with peace and hoped his sea turtle friend had found his way. He examined a flock of birds above the mast and the sounds of gulls echoed in his thoughts as the birds had a tendency to materialize from an empty sky when a kill had been made. He put in an extra bird for George. He took pleasure in the fact that he could help save that tiny life.

Turning the jawbone to its backside, he gazed at the angel who had come for George. He had etched her as just an outline to represent her ethereal presence. Quinn had thought of her often through the years but had never seen her again. Not even in his dreams. He wondered if his crimes against the earth were so dark that she would not come near. The purity of his memory of her made him feel ashamed.

The picture was finished and he twirled it back and forth. Making a decision, he stood and headed to the stern towards the Captain's stateroom. The man had shown kindness to the crew and respect to the animals they hunted. Knocking on the Captain's door, Quinn entered his office. "Sir, I would like you to have this."

The Captain studied the scrimshaw. "This is wonderful, Quinn.

One of the nicest pieces I have seen. Are you sure you do not want to keep it for yourself?"

Quinn looked down at the whale bone. So much blood, sweat and tears went into its creation. It was essentially the story of his life. He felt he had paid some sort of homage to the mother whale although he would always carry her scar upon his heart. "It would be my honor for you to accept this, sir."

"Thank you. I would like to place it on my personal box." The Captain looked at the seasoned whaler before him. "I will always value it."

Quinn brought an auger similar to the one that he had made for the doctor to drill holes into heads, and secured the picture to the wooden lid. As he bore through the bottom portion, a small lip of bone chipped off. He took the thin piece and decided he could use it as a new quill for the next project.

The New Shipmate

Quinn leaned forward into the blustery wind. Snow was gathering on the railings of the ship and the crew was constantly removing ice. The seas were too rough for any of the harpoon boats to chase the whales even if they were sighted. Even the Captain seemed to regret the decision to make a northern excursion this late in the year.

A sailor bumped into Quinn on the deck. The man appeared unsteady. Perhaps he was seasick. Some never really got over the feeling. Quinn recognized him as a recent hire who joined the crew during the last unloading of oil and bone near New York. "Are you alright?"

"I don't feel that well." The man coughed violently and bent over.

Quinn grabbed his shoulder and assisted him to the infirmary. "Doc, this man needs some help."

William helped the sick man from his jacket. He was sweating despite the frigid temperatures outside. "When did you come aboard?"

"Just a few days ago."

"Were you around anybody sick?" William felt a twinge of panic in his gut. Epidemics traveled like wildfire on a vessel.

"Well, my brother was not feeling well. I took the job in exchange for medicine. But I felt fine before we left." The man was looking increasingly pale.

"I want you to stay down below for now and don't touch anybody." The doctor ordered warm soup and isolation. He prayed that the man did not have the disease that was running through the inner cities. He had heard from his colleagues that a particular strong influenza was killing people in masses. If so, the entire boat may have been exposed. He got the job in exchange for medicine? The company should have known he would be a liability. "Is anybody else sick that you know of?" he addressed the question to Quinn.

"No, not that I know of." Quinn was surprised at the worry that clouded the older man's features.

"Alright, I need to inform the Captain that we could have a situation on our hands." William sent word that he needed to speak to one of the officers.

Quinn left the infirmary and crossed paths with the Captain coming down the deck. "Quinn, keep you scarf tight and don't let the cold under your jacket." The Captain almost tenderly arranged the woolen material and gave him a pat on the shoulder. He regarded the entire crew as his wards.

Within two days, Quinn woke with a fever. His head pounded and his chest was tight. He was dizzy when he got up from his bunk. "Pixie, I think I'm sick. Don't come near me or go into my room."

"Hell no!" the Cook exclaimed. The entire crew had been alerted to report any illness and rumor spread that several had already reported to the infirmary. "I'll be damned upset if you get sick. I need someone to boss around and share in my crazy excursions." His pulse quickened and he weakly smiled for encouragement as Quinn gathered some clothing and left the galley.

Quinn entered the doctors' office. "Bloody hell, not you too! I have at least eight other crewman sick." Dread filled the doctor's heart as Quinn presented himself to infirmary. The crew member from New York had died last night of respiratory failure. He was sure he had a full outbreak on his hands. "I'm sorry Quinn, but I have to isolate you with the rest."

Before he could say more, a worried deck hand appeared at the door. "Doc , you are needed in the Captain's quarters. He cannot get up from his bunk."

This was a nightmare. William grabbed his bag and went to the stateroom.

"How many are sick?" The Captain was older and the pain of breathing was rapidly overtaking him.

"At least nine men. The man who brought the disease on board died last night." The doctor quietly gave the information, knowing he was most likely telling the man of his impending death.

"Are you feeling okay, William?" The officer seemed to take the news in stride.

"So far I have tried to isolate everybody who is ill." The doctor could sense the dignified resignation in the old man's voice. "I will have to isolate myself as well soon."

"Do you need me to join the others?"

"Goodness no, you stay right here. I will bring you some medicine." The doctor returned to his office and retrieved the coca leaves from behind his desk. He thought of Quinn and their trip up the canyon to retrieve the plant. They had been jovial and discussed life, politics and women. He had a twinge of despair as he thought of his friend now isolated down below.

"Bloody hell, this cannot be happening." The doctor dashed back a cup of rum and returned to the Captain who ordered Avery to suspend all hunting and return to the shoreline.

Back in the bowels of the ship, Quinn was reminded of his first days on the boat years ago. Pain radiated in his head and spread down to his shoulders. He lay prone on the floor along with the other men, smelling the tar between the planks. He could not muster the energy to eat the soup that was delivered. The process of breathing was difficult and thoughts of George and his angel danced in his dreams. Would she soon be coming for him?

He struggled to breathe but pressure restricted him from fully expanding his lungs. A sharp pain in the side of his chest jerked him back to reality. He regained consciousness and realized he was on a table with William standing over him. Tears filled the older man's eyes and in all his years, Quinn realized he had never seen his friend cry.

"Can you breathe?" The doctor had inserted a needle apparatus between his ribs.

Quinn ruefully recognized the tool of one of his own designs. It was similar to a miniature harpoon. He smiled at the irony of having a spear plunged deep between his ribs. Somehow it seemed fitting. "Yes, it is a bit easier now."

"You are getting fluid around your lungs." William removed viscous liquid into a bowl.

Quinn looked up at his friend who had a rag of seawater tied around his face. Honestly, if it were not for the doctor and Pixie, he would have ended his life years ago. "I will be okay. Don't worry about me, William. You have truly been the reason I have continued living. You are a wonderful man and gifted healer and I will always love you for that. Make sure Pixie knows I love him as well."

"Don't talk that way. You are a fighter. You will make it." The doctor placed some of the coca leaf on his gum. "It has been my honor to call you my friend as well."

The doctor returned to his office, and removed his glasses. He dared not tell any of the men below that the Captain had perished. All but the most necessary of mechanics for sailing had been suspended as they raced homewards. William had quickly released the Captain's body to the sea with minimal crew at attendance. He could not risk contaminating any more people. Now his best friend lay dying down below. He started to cry at the thought of surrendering Quinn to the cold water.

Back in the hold, Quinn's chest quickly refilled with fluid. William's procedure helped slightly but he knew the inevitability of his destiny at this time. Men had already died around him. He was in such terrible physical pain. He smiled as he thought of Club and

George, the few balances against his own karmic scale. He thought he could hear whales calling to him. Their songs calmed him although they were mostly of sorrow. He had watched hundreds perish and could do nothing to save even one.

Gathering all the energy he had left, he crawled for the stairs. No one dared guard the entrance out of fear and he gained the deck without being noticed. The wind slapped him in the face as he removed his jacket. He was getting colder by the moment and soon could not feel his hands or feet as he crawled to the side of the ship. Staring off into the ocean mist, he thanked it for ushering him in. He watched the water beneath him and felt his vision cloud. Feeling a release, he dropped into the sea. He did not even feel the frigid water and consciously filled his lungs once submerged. Yes, he could hear the whales calling.

He was going home.

CHAPTER 22

Epilogue

I wiped my tears with a tissue and casually dropped it to the floor to join the rest of the wadded Kleenex. Although we had channeled many times over the months, this was by far one of the most emotional nights. "Quinn, I have to ask. Did the angel appear to you after you died?"

"She did appear to me near the end when I lay ill with the others," he confided in a soft whisper. "I was in so much pain. It hurt so much to breathe and blood was in my airways. Yet even then, there was fear of dying. I thought to myself, I am going to die here, and nobody will even know I existed. I felt my life had been stolen from me. I had been forced into life of carnage, one that I could never hope to erase the tarnish. I speak sadness for every animal's energy that we took."

Quinn was silent for a moment before speaking again. "When her light touched me, I looked away and said no. She was so pure, and I felt so unworthy. I felt I had to stay behind to help balance the karmic scale." Quinn spoke with incredible sadness.

"Who do you hope to reach with your story?"

"Everyone and anyone who will listen," Quinn continued. "You see, man is the most disrespectful animal on the planet. They will never stop or surrender. The whale will follow the path of the buffalo. I hope to ignite the heart energy in the depth of the human race. Compassion will be their only survivor, their only rescuer. I am hurting in my heart. I am hurting in my soul."

"Break!" Tim exclaimed and broke the trance, bringing his hands to his temples. "Wow, I could feel his death. I had to stop. He has such terrible pain. He feels so much guilt and responsibility. I don't know. Maybe the Collective can help heal him. I need you to take Quinn for a moment so I can speak to him directly."

I leaned back to begin meditating and Tim placed Quinn's energy onto my aura. "Quinn, I need to speak to you directly. The Collective was brought through an Inuit harpoon maker from a long lineage of family that even includes a woman. He has something to say to you."

Tim breathed slowly as he recalibrated to a new energy. "Quinn, my brother suffered a similar fate as your friend Jonas. He was struck with the blade as we hunted the walrus. I am apologetic in approach but you have faltered. The strike against your man is something that is part of our job. I agree that it is a terrible thing, but by being so upset at him, about him, you keep him from his journey to the light. Hold your right hand cupped, and place every bit of pain in your hand. Honor his presence and you will never forget him, but his essence needs to fly. On any heart moment, lift your hand and release. In his own journey, he can come back but not as the energy he is now. One, two, three, and let him fly upward into the light."

Tim released the Inuit and continued to speak to Quinn. "We have one little but large thing left to do. The energies of two whales are swimming below us. Prepare yourself for it is the mother and baby. I have isolated the baby away from its mother for a moment for they travel together. It is very draining to channel an animals' energy." He concentrated heavily for a moment. "She was okay. She followed her mother into the light. She is here to help release your energy Quinn. Don't block yourself. It is okay. You had no malice. Let it go. Cry and push it away. It changed your life. I, as the baby release your energy and forgive your action. You are free, no longer to be burdened by the thought of killing me. You are an extraordinary individual and I thank you for being upset. There were so many that did not care. Release your anguish, your shame, your responsibility, and anger. You have to let it go."

The room was silent for a few minutes as the session ended.

"Wow, I don't know if I can take any more," I said to my husband. I held up the empty container of tissue.

"I agree. I feel like a truck ran over me and then backed up again. But I think we helped him." Tim was done for the evening. "Yes, I am sure of it."

A few weeks later, we decided to channel Quinn again to ask him why he wanted us to share his story. This is what he said:

"I want to show what it was like to be alive in that time. The adventure, the deceit, the treasure, and the defeat. I realize in the end that I was not just human, but a creature of the earth like the ones that lay before me. I am so sure that whales possess an incredible camaraderie if accessed. They get angry, they get sad. They get happy and they are glad. I sensed this as I swung from my bosun chair with salt on my lips and grit in my ear. I worked hard so you could hear. I left myself on the bone as I wanted to be known."

"Thank you for telling my story. It is an unfortunate destiny which I hope will redeem itself in some way. Put it out and let them know. For when it is printed it will be time for me to go. I will rest forever and continue my journey. I must give toast to the souls of my mates and of the animals. I give them my heart and hope that they all rest for eternity. Father, please forgive me for I had no choice. I hope you understand that until now, I never had a voice."

Tranquility

copyright 1989 Richard M. Kohen
PINEKOHENS LTD

Connecting with The Collective

This story would not have been possible without the guidance of The Collective. Tim describes his process of channeling and his work with The Collective:

"Over the years, many spiritual guides have chosen to communicate with me. The Collective is a collection of many energies which have come together to provide wisdom, to shed light on hidden Truths. Although each feels their own, they collectively feel one way.

I access the Collective through meditation. My thoughts travel to a plane that I call "the ice field"—something like a frozen lake with fishing holes through its expanse. Each opening allows the passage of information, like ethereal fiber optics. The Collective facilitates my access to this information.

In our travels, we have come across many energies who are lost. Some energies do not even realize they have passed from their earth life. Others have chosen to stay. Most are stuck, but it is not as simple as just telling them to "go to the light" for they do not know the way. The Collective allows us to help guide these entities to complete their journey home.

As we connected with Quinn over the years he became like family to us. Through the telling of his story, I believe he has found peace and will depart in the company of the angel. He has learned from us, and we have learned from him. I can only hope he will continue to assist us on another energetic plane."

This is the first book of our combined efforts with the Collective. We hope you will join us as we embark on more adventures.